Mind Games

USA TODAY BESTSELLING AUTHOR

T.K. LEIGH

MIND GAMES

Published by Carpe Per Diem, Inc. / Tracy Kellam, 25852 McBean Parkway # 806, Santa Clarita, CA 91355

Edited by: Kim Young, Kim's Editing Services

Cover Image Elements:

Merla© 2019

Used under license from Adobe

To making the most of a canceled flight…

Chapter One

HAVE YOU EVER wondered what would have happened if Alice never saw the White Rabbit and followed him into Wonderland? If Cinderella never found the courage to walk into that ball all alone and dance with Prince Charming? If Ariel hadn't gone to the surface and saved Prince Eric from drowning, even though everyone warned her about humans?

One moment. One decision. One life forever changed because they opted for one path over another. It's remarkable to think our choices have this much power, this much ability to alter the course our lives had been on.

I've often imagined what my life would look like had I chosen differently. Different college. Different profession. Different love. It's one of those things that keeps us up in the wee hours of the night, contemplating deep thoughts we have no control over, since the likelihood of getting a second chance is doubtful.

At least that's what I've always thought… Until a trip to Las Vegas for a bachelorette party brought me back to that proverbial fork in the road. One I didn't know existed.

* * *

"Are you girls seriously not coming to the club with us tonight?" Bernadette whines over the loud, jarring noise of the busy casino. Her bright red lips form into a pout as she looks at Chloe and me.

When she'd first proposed celebrating Hannah's bachelorette party in Vegas, I looked forward to getting out of Manhattan for a weekend in Sin City, especially in January. But after only twenty-four hours, I longed for the sounds and smells of New York. Now that I've been here going on four nights, I'm all but counting down the minutes until I can board that plane. In a little more than twelve hours, I get to do just that.

"We have an early flight tomorrow," Chloe responds.

Out of the entire bridal party, we're the only two who seem to have commitments and obligations back home. Not only are we leaving a day earlier than everyone else, we're using it as an excuse not to have to suffer through yet another night at yet another club. A darkened room reeking of sweat, alcohol, and perfume. Ridiculously loud music. Barely any space to move or dance. It isn't my idea of a fun evening out.

"I thought your flight wasn't until one or two," Bernadette argues back.

"We still have to get to the airport on time. We don't have the luxury of sleeping in all day like you do."

Bernadette opens her mouth, presumably to continue stating her case, when Hannah steps forward, wrapping her arms around Chloe. "I'm so glad you took the time to come." Pulling back, she gives her a sincere smile before hugging me. "Don't worry. I get it," she whispers. "If I could, I'd be right there with you."

She drops her hold on me, and the three of us share a conspiratorial look, like we did as kids when we were up to something.

Growing up, we were three peas in a pod. We lived in the same neighborhood and were practically inseparable. Hell, I remember many summer days giggling about our dream weddings to our dream guys. Hannah always fantasized about marrying a successful doctor, one who loves kids as much as she does. Now, she's mere weeks away from marrying that successful doctor.

"Come on." She spins from us, looping her arm through Bernadette's. "I'm a bit parched."

Several of the other bridal party members whistle and cheer as they retreat from the lobby, on their way to one of the many clubs. As they're about to get swallowed up by the hectic casino atmosphere, Hannah glances over her shoulder, blowing both of us a kiss. We return it, as we always do.

Chloe and I wait until they disappear from view, then exhale simultaneously.

"Well, thank god that's over." She starts toward the bank of elevators, her strides purposeful. "I swear, if one more guy approaches me thinking I'm a prostitute because my hair's a different shade, I'm going to lose it. I'm not the first person to color my hair gray and lilac, for crying out loud." She gestures to her wavy locks that fall to her mid-back.

I must admit, it took me a while to get used to the color, knowing I'd never be so bold as to change my hair to such a unique tone. But that's Chloe. Daring and a bit reckless. Plus, her natural shade of blonde makes it easier to do something like that. There's not much I can do with my nearly jet-black hair. As far as our appearance goes, Chloe and I are as opposite as can

3

be. She's short and petite, the picture of an all-American girl, aside from her choice in hair color. I'm on the taller side with curves and olive-toned skin, thanks to my Latina heritage.

"You know how this place can be," I respond when I catch up to her. "It's bachelorette party central. You saw how the girls behaved. They're away from home and responsibility so they decided to throw common sense out the window and flirt with anything with a pulse. Same goes for the men here for bachelor parties. And, as we all know, men aren't nearly as intelligent as women, so they say and do even dumber things."

Her laughter fills the elevator vestibule, overpowering the abrasive noise of the casino. "You've got that right." When a car arrives, she slings her arm over my shoulders, which proves slightly difficult due to our height difference, her five-two to my five-seven, but we manage. Like always.

"Lobby tomorrow at eleven?" I arch a brow at Chloe when the elevator stops on my floor.

Another reason I get along so well with her. While the rest of the bridal party insisted on cramming eight people into two rooms, we refused to take any part in that. The only thing that made this trip bearable was that I had my own space.

"Or maybe I should tell you 10:30 so you'll be on time."

She playfully jabs me in the side. "Don't worry. I'll be there. There's no way in hell I'm missing my flight out of this godforsaken town."

"Good. Or I'm leaving without you. Because there's no way in hell *I'm* missing my flight out of this godforsaken town."

"Goodnight, Izzy," she sings, pushing me out of the car before the doors close on me.

"Night, Chloe," I call back as I make my way toward my room.

Once inside, I take a minute to relish in the tranquility. My ears still ring from the constant barrage of noise in the casino, but other than a faint conversation I can make out from the room next door as the occupants get ready for a night out, it's peaceful, the whirring of the air conditioner the only sound.

An urgent need to wash off the remnants of tonight's festivities, namely the showgirl lessons that came complete with full makeup, overtakes me and I head for the bathroom, starting the shower.

A few minutes later, after scrubbing my face rigorously, I feel like myself again. Not this dress-wearing, club-going girl I've been the past few days so Hannah could have the bachelorette party she deserved. Though I suspect this was more the type of bachelorette party Bernadette, her older sister, would want. Hannah would have preferred a quiet weekend in Wine Country. Hell, knowing Hannah, she would have preferred a weekend where we all volunteered at the inner-city schools.

Emerging from the bathroom, I glance at the clock to see it's just after eleven. I should pack and get some sleep, but I'm not even close to being tired. As a nurse, I typically work the night shift. After staying out until the early hours of the morning all weekend, my body has remained on that schedule. So, instead of throwing on some pajamas, I slide on a pair of jeans and a black top, then leave my room to explore the Vegas nightlife on my own. And hopefully find a low-key bar. After a weekend of nothing but overpriced, pretentious clubs, I need a simple bar and a good beer.

Most other women my age probably wouldn't want to venture off on their own at night in Vegas, but I'm not most women. I like being alone. Like being able to do what I want when I want. Like not having to depend on anyone else for my own happiness. That's the benefit of being an only child. An *adopted* only child. I became fiercely independent at an early age.

I meander along the casino floor, the tables overflowing with people trying their hand at blackjack, poker, or roulette, probably gambling away their life savings in the hopes of winning big. Cocktail waitresses in skintight dresses that barely cover their ass carry trays holding drinks. Despite having one of the top air filtration systems available, a thin layer of smoke seems to fill the space, the stench of nicotine permanently ingrained in my nostrils. It's going to take days to get the stink out of my hair once I get home.

As I wander in search of a place where I can grab a decent beer, the sound of live music cuts through, a nice change from the typical thump of club music they blare all hours of the day. I look in its direction, spying what appears to be an Irish pub. I grin at the familiarity. My mother would admonish me for going to an Irish pub while in Vegas, considering I live in New York and we can't trip without falling on yet another pub just like this one. That's probably what calls me to this place. It reminds me of home.

I step inside, everything about my surroundings seeming to go against what Vegas stands for. Yes, it's still a bar and the music is loud, but it's not ostentatious. Not filled with women wearing as little clothing as they can get away with on the prowl for some poor schmuck to buy them overpriced drinks for the night. Not crawling with men dressed in suits who bathed in far too much cologne.

I walk toward a long bar that sits along the wall and find a vacant stool. My eyes are drawn to the ceiling, dozens of bills of every currency pinned to it. A bartender approaches and takes my order for a beer, returning with a pint within seconds. I take a sip of the hoppy ale, exhaling at the flavor that seems so foreign after the past few nights of only consuming mixed, saccharine drinks. This is exactly what I need to feel normal again.

I survey the darkened space, nothing flashy or unique about it. Just like every other bar I've been to in my adult life, the lounge is filled with heavy wood tables, patrons enjoying a variety of beers and bar food while they listen to live music. A large crowd fills the empty area in front of the stage, dancing to the band as they cover a Coldplay song. They're pretty good, much better than some of the artists I hear on the radio these days. I'll take rock music any day over the latest auto-tuned boy band who wouldn't know how to hold a guitar if their life depended on it.

The song ends and applause breaks out, a few girls cheering and clapping enthusiastically. Déjà vu washes over me, like I've been here before. In a way, I have. I was once one of those exuberant fans cheering for the local band, hoping they'd someday make it big. But that was a lifetime ago.

Shaking off the memories, I turn my attention back to my beer, perusing the menu the bartender left for me.

"Thanks all," the lead singer's voice carries over the loud chatter and clanging of ice against glass. "We're going to take a quick break, but before we do, we have a special guest who's agreed to get up on stage with us tonight. Remember this name because in the next few months, you won't be able to turn on your radios without hearing his music. Ladies and gentlemen, give it up for Asher York."

A gasp escapes, my eyes darting toward the stage. I freeze, my brain unable to tell my lungs to breathe, my heart to beat, my body to move. All I hear is that name. It can't be him, can it? How? I've never been great at statistics, but the likelihood of the two of us being in the same bar in Las Vegas has to be... What? One in a million? A billion? It must be someone else with the same name. Someone else who's also a musician. Someone else who's six-two, with dark hair and a smile that can melt panties.

I tell myself I'm imagining it, that I'm still stuck in the memories of my college days when my friends and I would go to whatever club Asher's band was playing and dance the night away. That must be it. The reality of being in the same room as him seems so far out of the realm of possibilities, especially considering the last I knew, he was a music teacher in the suburbs of Boston, playing the occasional gig on the weekends.

Then again, the last time I spoke to him was eight years ago.

A lot can change in that amount of time.

And when a figure jumps onto the stage and faces the crowd, I realize truer words have never been spoken, or thought. A lot *can* change in that amount of time. And Asher York has certainly changed.

I watch with a mixture of intrigue and surprise as he grabs an acoustic-electric guitar from a stand, plugging a cable into the end of the body. The man resembles the Asher York I once knew, but he's a far cry from the lanky man I remember. His broad chest pulls at the simple gray t-shirt, his biceps filling the sleeves quite nicely. His dark hair is no longer perfectly groomed. It's grown out and has a sexy, disheveled vibe, the perfect complement to the scruff along his jaw. But that's not the biggest change. Oh no. As if he weren't rock god personified with the longer hair and muscular physique, he has to add tattoos to the fantasy.

I've always found Asher York attractive. But now... He is all man. Manly man. And when his voice fills the bar, sending an involuntary shiver down my spine, it's somehow deeper and more enthralling than I remember. And I definitely remember him. Asher York isn't the kind of person anyone could forget.

I should leave. Pay for my beer. Head back to my room. The last thing I need is to reopen old wounds. And seeing Asher does just that. But like the first time my college roommate dragged me to a club to see a local band that was gaining in popularity, I'm drawn to the man's rough, emotion-filled voice.

I stare at my beer, concentrating on the melody. It sounds familiar, like a cloudy memory trying to return to the surface of my subconscious. The longer I listen, the more clear it becomes. By the time he sings the first chorus, it hits me. It's the same melody I'd heard him toil over endlessly during those late summer nights we stayed up together at his grandmother's lake house, while my boyfriend, then fiancé slept inside.

Who also happened to be Asher's brother.

During the two years I dated Jessie, I was welcomed into his family with open arms. That included spending a few weeks of the summer at the lake house. It was actually one of the things I missed most when we broke up. The card games. The smell of burgers on the grill. Spending the early morning hours listening to Asher pluck away at his guitar as he attempted to piece together a song.

This song.

Allowing my hair to cascade in front of my face in the hopes that Asher doesn't recognize me in the crowd, I risk a glance at him. He seems to have cast a spell on everyone here, just as he did all those years ago. People bob their heads in time with the song, one I've heard more times than I care to admit, the familiar chords akin to coming home after a long absence.

I'm transfixed as I listen to him sing about feeling like he was made for a particular woman, but she never saw him until it was too late. I don't realize my eyes are glued to his every move until deafening applause thunders around me. The girls who preened before the lead singer of the other band mere minutes ago now fawn over Asher.

He smiles that breathtaking smile of his as he thanks the audience, still as enigmatic a presence as always. His gaze floats over the crowd, coming to an abrupt stop when he locks eyes with mine. I try to look away, but the simple act of our gazes meeting has turned me to stone, apart from the fluttering in my chest. It shouldn't. I shouldn't have any reaction to him.

Just like I shouldn't have tried to kiss him mere hours after I ended things with his brother all those years ago.

Snapping out of my stupor, I refocus my attention on my beer and drain it. I grab a bill from my wallet and leave it on the counter, not caring about getting any change. The excessive tip is a price I'm willing to pay to avoid having to talk to Asher, considering the last time I saw him I pretended to have no memory of the previous night and our almost-kiss.

I'm about to jump down from the stool when a hand on the bar next to me stops me.

"Running off without saying hi?"

My eyes dart up, coming face-to-face with Asher York. His voice is even smoother than I remember. A low rumble that hits places on my body that haven't felt excitement in an eternity.

I part my lips, attempting to come up with a response, but I'm rendered speechless when I catch a glimpse of his arm leaning on the bar, the position causing his biceps to flex and push against the confines of his t-shirt, stretching the fabric.

A woodsy scent surrounds me as I stare, the smell reminding me of large family dinners, playing guitar on the dock overlooking the lake on his grandmother's property, roasting marshmallows. Reminds me of a girl I used to be. One I've tried to keep in the past.

Swallowing down the bittersweet memories, I push a strand of hair behind my ear, forcing a smile. "Asher. Good to see you." I hold my head high, looking anywhere but directly into his eyes. I can't. He has the same eyes as Jessie. Born eleven months apart, their appearance was always strikingly similar. But that was where their similarities ended, the two brothers as opposite as two people can be. Regardless, I've never met two siblings as close as they are. Or maybe I found it so foreign since I'm an only child.

"Phew." He blows out a breath, laughing shakily. "I wasn't positive it was you. I thought it was, but everyone in this town seems to look like someone else."

I shrug, finally meeting his gaze. "It's me."

"Good. That would have been awkward otherwise." A flirtatious smile curves up the corners of his lips. He even has the same smile as Jessie. But Asher's looks more natural, like he's actually happy. "What are you doing in Vegas?" he continues when I don't immediately say anything.

"I could ask you the same question."

He nods at the stage. "Music." He doesn't embellish. "Your turn."

"Bachelorette party. Hannah's getting married next month, and Bernadette was in charge of planning her bachelorette party."

A look of understanding crosses his face. "Say no more."

As uneasy as it should be to see Asher again, considering his connection to a time in my life I'd prefer to keep in my rearview mirror, it's refreshing to talk to someone who already knows me, scars and all. Someone I don't have to go into all the details of my life with because they already know.

"Cash you out, miss?" The bartender's voice cuts through.

I nod. "Thank you."

"Actually," Asher interrupts before the bartender can retreat with my money, "she'll have another. And I'll have an IPA." He places a finger on the cash I'd left on the bar and slides it back in front of me. "Put all her drinks on my tab."

"That's not necessary," I insist, attempting to push the bill back toward the bartender. "I really should be going. It's been a long night and I—"

The heat coming off him as his hand wraps around my arm stops me mid-sentence. I fling my wide eyes to his, my insides vibrating at his touch. Something that never happened when his brother touched me, caressed me, made love to me. That should have been a sign back then, but I was too young to realize it. Too smitten by the handsome college senior who noticed me. Or maybe I just didn't care. Maybe I'd wanted to feel like I was wanted, like I was cherished.

"Stay."

One word, and my mouth goes dry.

One word, and my heart pounds in my chest.

One word, and I forget all the reasons I should leave.

"Okay." I slowly slink back into my barstool.
What harm can one drink with an old friend do?

Chapter Two

"**S**O YOU QUIT without a backup plan?" I ask several hours later as Asher and I sip on our beers, the bartender having just announced last call.

I'd told myself I'd only stay for one drink. One drink soon turned into three as I caught him up on everything that's been going on in my life. How I ended up getting my master's, something I never would have done if I'd married Jessie. Hell, before I broke off our engagement, I probably would have been happy working at a general practitioner's office where the hours were normal and the stress level low. But something about the breakup made me reevaluate my plans and think about what I really wanted. So I continued with my education, focusing on pediatric oncology. The hours are less than optimal, the mental strain of holding these precious young lives in my hands high, not to mention the heartbreak when I lose a patient, but I can't imagine doing anything else.

"If I wanted to pursue my dreams, I didn't want anything holding me back. My teaching job was a crutch. I turned down gigs because I couldn't take time off from work. *Good* gigs, too. A few opening up for Dave Matthews Band, Ed Sheeran, Jason Mraz. Granted, I would have been the first opener when everyone was waiting in line for beer, but it was still a great gig I had to miss because it was during the week and my headache of a principal refused to sign off on the time. Thought it was a waste. So about four years ago, when I needed to either start my master's so I could keep teaching or do something else, I decided to take the leap and do something else."

I drain the remainder of my drink, then sip on some water. "That takes some serious *cojones*. I don't know many people who would quit their job and move to Los Angeles to chase their dreams."

"What can I say? I'm not most people." He playfully nudges me. "You should realize that by now."

"I certainly do."

There's a warmth within his gaze when I lift my eyes to meet his. But there's something more, too. Something that's been missing from my life all these years.

I clear my throat, breaking through the mounting tension I'm convinced is one-sided. "Weren't you scared?"

"I was." He looks forward, staring into the distance, squinting. "But I was more scared of never pursuing my dreams. Of being content with a life that was just good enough. Don't get me wrong," he adds quickly. "I loved my job. Loved teaching kids about music and seeing the joy on their faces when they nailed that difficult passage for the first time. But I always looked at teaching as something I could do to pay the bills while I pursued my dreams. So when teaching got in the way of those dreams, I knew what I had to do."

I smile a genuine smile, one that reaches my eyes and warms my heart. "That's incredible. And inspiring."

"It hasn't all been easy. Sure, they call Los Angeles the city of dreams..." He shakes his head, sipping on his beer. "Believe me. It's not."

"But you made it work."

The corners of his mouth quirk up. "I have."

15

The lights snap on, the universal sign of the bartender saying, "You don't have to go home, but you can't stay here." I check my watch, surprised to see it's practically two and that we've been talking for nearly three hours. I can't remember the last time I've been so immersed in another person that I lost all concept of time. It was probably at the lake house when Asher and I would end up staying awake all night without either of us realizing it, too lost in the music he strummed.

"I guess that's our cue to leave," he remarks, finishing his beer.

"I suppose it is."

I slide off my barstool, but my heel catches on a leg, propelling me forward. Asher reacts quickly, wrapping an arm around my waist and pulling me upright...directly into his body.

His warm, firm body.

Every inch of me instantly buzzes to life as a thrilling sensation washes over me, leaving me nearly breathless. This isn't the first time Asher's held me. Hell, it's not the first time he's broken my fall, preventing me from making a complete fool out of myself. But it's never felt like this. Like my insides are ready to ignite from the electricity coursing through me.

I tilt my head back and peer into his eyes that glisten under the bright lights of the bar. His chest expands a little more with every inhale. The motion is subtle, but I notice it. Just like I notice the swipe of his tongue along his bottom lip, moistening them. The slight flaring of his nostrils. The awe and curiosity in his stare. Does he feel this, too?

"You okay?"

Eyes the shade of whiskey skate over my frame before returning to mine. He makes no immediate move to drop his hold on me. In fact, he seems to draw me even

16

closer, his fingers thrumming against the exposed flesh between my jeans and top, his touch a ray of sun on that first spring-like day. So unexpected. So surprising. Yet still very welcome.

"Izzy?" he presses when I don't immediately respond, lost in the tremors the mere sensation of his arms wrapped around me kindles. His voice pulls me back to the present, reminding me who I am. Who he is.

Just like he reminded me all those years ago.

I push out of his embrace, increasing the distance. "Those beers must have caught up to me. I should have eaten something."

I smooth my hands over my shirt, pulling it down so no more skin shows around my waistband. Fidgeting with the hem, I rock on my heels, the way he's staring at me unnerving, like he can read my thoughts and is about to recite a list of reasons we can never be together. I am more than aware of those reasons. I don't need a recap of them.

"Well..." I scramble to push past him. "It was good seeing you. Thanks for the beers."

I hold my breath as I make my escape, about to ring the victory bell when I hear his voice call out, "Want to grab a bite to eat?"

I come to an abrupt stop, blinking. I slowly glance over my shoulder. "What was that?"

He averts his gaze, scraping a hand through his hair. Asher's never been the nervous type. More brooding, mysterious, aloof. I'd lost count of the number of girls I'd witnessed fawning over him whenever his band had a gig. But he never seemed to notice them.

"Sorry. I don't know what I was thinking. I just enjoyed spending time with you again and wasn't ready

17

to say goodbye yet. But you're right. You probably should—"

"Yes," I interrupt before he can finish his statement.

His brows furrow. "Excuse me?"

I fully face him. "Yes, I'd like to grab a bite to eat. With you."

"Are you sure? You're not too tired?"

I pass him a sardonic look. "Were you not paying attention to a single word I said tonight? I'm a nurse. My body's used to staying up late."

A dazzling smile flashes across his features. "So you're still a night owl? Even all these years later?"

I shrug. "Guilty as charged."

"Well then…" Approaching, he extends his arm toward the exit. "Shall we?"

"We shall." I make my way onto the casino floor, which is even busier than it was earlier. It doesn't seem to faze these people that it's after two in the morning. They're still slamming back drinks, which causes them to be more reckless with their money.

I've never been a gambler. Hell, I don't think I've so much as put a single bill into a slot machine the entire time I've been here. Living in Manhattan with the high rent doesn't give me much wiggle room to throw away money on frivolities.

I allow Asher to take the lead through the casino, but make sure to keep some space between us. Regardless, there's still a buzz in the air. As we pass a group of men in their twenties dressed in dark shirts and jeans, their hair slicked back, their musky cologne overpowering, a few of them eye me up and down, lasciviously licking their lips.

Asher steps closer and rests his hand on my lower back, his protective nature flaring. "You really should be careful walking around this place at night. Especially alone." He narrows his disapproving gaze on me, which is riddled with concern.

"I can take care of myself." I roll my eyes. "And for the record... I walk around Manhattan at night all the time."

"I'm more than aware you can take care of yourself, Iz. If I remember correctly, there was an incident at one of the festivals our band played where you managed to bring some schmuck who attempted to hit on you to his knees. It was the highlight of the gig."

I laugh, surprised at his memory of one particular performance when he's played hundreds, maybe even thousands. Then again, he *is* an artist. He crafts beautiful melodies with heartfelt lyrics. He probably remembers everything about everyone, pulling inspiration from everywhere he can.

"You still remember that?"

"How could I forget? It was all anyone talked about for weeks. About how tiny Isabella Nolan took down the star quarterback."

"What can I say? My father refused to send me away to college unless I took self-defense classes. When that prick wouldn't take no for an answer and tried to make a move on me, I knew exactly how to send him to his knees. There's nothing as effective as an open palm to the nose and a knee in the groin to knock out your opponent." I playfully waggle my brows, following him outside to the valet stand, where he hands a ticket to an attendant.

The instant I step into the chilly night air, a shiver rolls through me. I rub my arms. While the temperature has been above average for January, according to several of the locals I've spoken to, nighttime is still on the cooler side. When I'd dressed earlier, I hadn't expected to go outside. I didn't expect to run into Asher York, either, yet here I am.

"Take this." He shrugs out of his leather jacket and places it over my shoulders, leaving himself in just a t-shirt. A few women in tight dresses whistle as they walk past, ogling him.

I'd like to say seeing his muscular arms doesn't have the same effect on me, but it would be a lie. His physique is one you can't help but admire. Not too bulky, yet not just skin and bones, either. His arms are ones you crave to have wrapped around you. Arms you hurry home to after a long day. Arms you subconsciously seek out in the middle of the night as you sleep peacefully.

"Thanks," I say in a small voice, tugging his jacket closer, savoring the warmth. I inhale deeply, the material smelling like Asher — a woodsy, citrus scent. It's refreshing to know some things never change.

"Only out in the desert does it go from eighty degrees during the day to the forties and fifties at night." He looks up to the sky, the stars barely visible against the bright lights of Vegas. On a long exhale, he returns his eyes to mine. "But it beats all the snowstorms back east."

"You've got that right. The last few winters have been rough. I've lost count of the number of times I slept at the hospital so I wouldn't miss my shift. Or so I wouldn't have to try to find my way home in the middle of a blizzard."

"It's been that bad?"

I nod. "We've had some big storms that dropped upwards of a foot, sometimes more. If it's only a few inches, it's not that bad. But when we get that much snow, the city has trouble keeping up with shoveling and plowing, especially where I live."

"And where's that?"

"Tribeca. It's—"

"I know where it is. Jessie..." He stops short, wide eyes flinging to mine.

It's the first time either of us have brought him up, our very own elephant in the room. I've thought of Jessie throughout the night. How could I not when spending time with Asher? But now that his name is out there, an awkward tension has made itself known, coiling around and squeezing the life out of what, mere minutes ago, was a fun, lighthearted evening.

"I mean..." He stammers, trying to recover, apprehensive about Jessie's presence between us. "I played a few gigs in the city before I moved out west."

A small ball of guilt lodges in my stomach. We've both moved on, both dated other people. But those other people weren't his older brother. His own flesh and blood. Granted, Asher and I *aren't* dating, nor will we ever, but I know how Jessie is. He'll grow suspicious if he learns Asher was with me, even if merely as a friend. Just like I know Asher's struggling with his own thoughts of betrayal.

"Here we are," Asher announces, his voice brightening. Perhaps out of relief.

I look up to see a classic red Mustang convertible rounding the corner. "Is that *yours*?" I blink repeatedly, gaping at the stunning vehicle rumbling our way, the beautiful purr of the engine like a siren's call.

"And if it is?"

"That car is..." I shake my head. "Wow. My dad would lose his shit if he learned you were driving one. And by lose his shit, I mean he'd try to con you out of it. It's... What? A sixty-five?"

"Sixty-four."

"Damn. My dad would *definitely* try to con you out of it."

I follow him toward the passenger side, my eyes soaking in the beauty before me. And I'm not the only one. Every male within the vicinity has stopped, their attention drawn to the sleek lines of the car instead of their dates. It's not something you see every day.

"He always did have a thing for old cars, didn't he?" Asher holds my elbow, helping me into the passenger seat before making his way around to the driver's side. "Want me to put the top up?"

"I'll be fine. I should take advantage of the fresh air while I can, even if it is a little chilly."

He slides into his seat with ease, pressing his foot against the clutch before shifting into first. I tug his jacket tighter around my body, the wind cutting against my face. But I wouldn't trade this moment for anything. Hair whipping in front of me. The Vegas lights blinking all around me. And Asher York sitting beside me. It's a completely unexpected turn of events. Then again, the best things in life often are.

"Are you sure you're okay?" Asher shouts over the noise of the wind and engine as he merges onto the interstate. "I can pull over and put up the top."

"I'm fine," I yell back. "But I thought we were going to get something to eat."

"We are." He flashes me a devious grin before returning his attention to the road.

"Where? The Strip is—"

"Do you think all this town has to offer is located on Las Vegas Boulevard?"

I shrug. "Pretty much."

"Trust me. There are a few hidden gems."

"Is that where you're taking me? To a hidden gem?"

"Absolutely. A hidden gem for a hidden gem."

Chapter Three

"THEY HAVE RED velvet pancakes?" Excitement oozes from my voice as I scan the menu that seems to have everything someone looking for a post-bar snack could ask for.

I've been to my fair share of late-night diners. This place is like a late-night diner on steroids. Red velvet pancakes. Amaretto french toast. Hell, if you wanted to go big, you could get a filet mignon. Even the ambience is a far cry from the grungy diners I'm used to. It's more reminiscent of a trendy supper club from back in the day. In fact, it probably was. Booths line the walls, white cloth-covered tables filling the rest of the open space. The lighting is on the dark side, all the windows tinted, presumably to make everyone forget that dawn is slowly approaching. As would be expected in this town, the bar serves alcohol twenty-four/seven.

Viva Las Vegas.

"And they are delicious," Asher comments. "In fact, you can't go wrong here. Everything they serve is incredible."

"So you come here often?" I ask in a fake seductive voice, grateful we're back to the way things have always been with us. Light. Fun. Easy. No more talking about Jessie.

"Actually, I do."

His response piques my interest. "Do you play a lot of gigs out here?"

"You could say that," he answers after a moment of contemplation.

"How long of a drive is it from LA?"

He brushes his thumb along his chin, looking into the distance before shifting his eyes back to mine. "About four hours. Depending on traffic."

"Kind of like living in the Tri-state area."

"It's even worse in LA. At least in New York, the public transportation system is great. You could just hop on Metro-North."

"Which is what I do, since it only takes… What? An hour?"

"No such luck in LA. If you want to get anywhere in the area, you're stuck driving."

"There's no subway system at all?"

"There's the metro, but it's not convenient and doesn't go everywhere most people need it to. It's nowhere near as convenient and widespread as the subway in New York. Or the T up in Boston." A hint of his accent slips in when his mouth caresses the name of the city he once called home. It was never overpowering or annoying, as was the case with some of the guys I met when I moved to Boston for college. It's subtle, an acknowledgment of his roots. One I hope he never loses.

"Well…" I lean back into the booth. "At least you have an incredible car to be stuck in traffic in."

"I can't complain about that. Actually, I—"

"Here are your drinks," our petite blonde waitress interrupts, placing a Bloody Mary in front of me and a coffee in front of Asher.

I felt a little guilty ordering an alcoholic drink, since he's not drinking, but I needed something to take the edge off after the way my body reacted to his arms around me. And the Bloody Marys coming out of the

24

bar looked too good to pass up. Shrimp. Bacon. Blue cheese-stuffed olives. It's a drink that was made for me.

"Are you ready to place your orders?"

"I am," Asher replies confidently, without even opening the menu to peruse the options. Then he looks at me. "Do you know what you'd like?"

I close my menu, holding it toward our waitress. "I can't resist. Red velvet pancakes."

"Good choice," she assures me before shifting her attention to Asher. "And for you?" She bats her lashes, her smile turning from polite to coquettish when she steals a glance at his tattoo-covered arms.

I never thought I'd be the type of girl who'd be interested in a guy with tattoos. I certainly shouldn't be interested in *this* one. But I can't dismiss the pang of jealousy rolling through me at the thought of this stranger ogling Asher. I try to tell myself it's because he's a friend, that I want what's best for him and this woman isn't it. But that didn't cause me to be jealous of anyone Asher dated while I was with Jessie. I'd even attempted to set him up with one of the girls in my dorm, thinking they'd be perfect for each other. She was a music major with a voice that was a combination of Adele and P!nk. I had listened to her go on about how great of a kisser he was, how much she loved his body. Not one flare of jealousy. But now, the mere idea of someone flirting with Asher has me glowering, judging everything about this complete stranger when I normally don't judge anyone.

He orders steak and eggs, which includes a filet mignon instead of a skirt steak, as is the case at most diners. The waitress lingers a few extra seconds, smiling coyly at Asher. Then she spins from us, and I can't help but think she's swaying her hips a little more than necessary.

25

"She wants you," I observe once she's a safe distance away. I take a much-needed sip of my Bloody Mary, which is as delicious as it looks.

"No, she doesn't." He pours a bit of milk into his coffee, skipping the sweetener altogether. Just like I remember. It's comforting to know some things haven't changed. "She was just being friendly. Probably hoping for a good tip."

"Right…," I say in a drawn-out voice, rolling my eyes. Speaking of things that never change…

It didn't matter how blatant the girls who fawned all over him were. He always brushed them off. He dated, but he never seemed to have the same passion about any of them as he did his music.

"Your girlfriend must hate going to your gigs, knowing the women in the audience will drool all over you." I swipe the condensation off the side of my glass.

He rests his forearms on the table between us, leaning toward me. His eyes darken, almost leering. The light, carefree atmosphere we've enjoyed since we arrived here vanishes. My gaze locks with his, meeting that same wanton stare he'd regarded me with as he held me in his arms. But this time it's even more pronounced. More shameless. More devious.

"What makes you say that?" he asks in a low tone, swiping his tongue along his bottom lip.

My core clenches, blood rushing to my cheeks. This reaction is so wrong. On so many levels. But there's no denying the hunger bubbling within me. The electricity sparking in the air between us. As much as I want to blame it on the lack of male companionship over the past few months, I can't. I know the truth. That my body has always acted this way around Asher. I just didn't want to acknowledge it for what it was. What it still is. A connection even the passing of years couldn't fracture. In fact, it's only made it stronger.

"I—" I stammer, fumbling for a response that doesn't give away how out of sorts I am.

"Oh, come now. I've never known you to be tongue-tied, Isabella," he remarks smoothly, a different side of Asher. "Tell me." His voice turns gruff, causing the hairs on my nape to stand on end. My heart rate increases. My head becomes foggy. The background noise fades away, like this is a dream. Maybe it is.

Maybe I fell asleep after showering and Asher York manifested in my dreams for some reason. Just like Ebenezer Scrooge was convinced his manifestation of Jacob Marley was due to something he ate, perhaps this fantasy of spending a night in Vegas with Asher York is the result of too much liquor and not enough food.

"Why do you think our waitress wants me?" he presses, his eyes focusing more intently on me.

I consider a viable response. I could list the obvious signs that would cause even a blind person to realize they're getting hit on. Instead, I test my limits. If this is a manifestation, a dream, what do I have to lose?

"Because if our situation were reversed, I'd act the same way," I admit, the words leaving me before I have a chance to evaluate the potential ramifications of being so truthful. My statement rings around us as I stare, seconds ticking by in a savage march. I feel like a contestant on one of those talent shows waiting to hear whether they'll continue on to the following week or be sent home, their dreams of stardom dashed. That's the power Asher holds over me at this very moment.

Hope seems to build in his gaze, his eye contact strong, his lips parting slightly. He leans closer, the corners of his mouth quirking up, as if struggling to reel

27

it in but can't. As if he's waited years for me to say something like this.

Then, just as quickly as his bright expression appears, it fades, gaze distant and even. As stoic as a soldier. "Thankfully, that's not an issue."

"You're right." I swallow down the pain of disappointment rising through my body, forcing the most fabricated smile of my life. If Asher can tell it's fake, he doesn't bring it up. "It's not."

With a shaky hand, I grab my Bloody Mary, taking a long sip. The spicy drink tingles as it hits my tongue and throat, but I've had spicier food. Hell, my mother jokes she pureed jalapeños and spoon-fed them to me as a baby to toughen me up.

"Not that." When he grabs my free hand, I fling my eyes to his, loosening the desperate grip my lips have on my straw. I remain silent, awaiting further explanation. "I'm talking about my girlfriend coming to one of my gigs. *That's* not an issue."

I perk up. "Oh?"

A sexy smirk draws on his full mouth and he releases his hold on me, angling away. "No girlfriend."

I nod, pretending the information is inconsequential. Inwardly, my libido does a little victory dance. I attempt to settle her down, tell her this doesn't change anything, but the sex-starved nymph refuses to listen.

"And your boyfriend wouldn't like it if he learned you were here with me at, oh…" He looks at his watch, "three in the morning."

"That's not an issue, either."

He raises a single brow. "Oh?"

"No boyfriend."

He makes a subtle gesture of acknowledgment by pursing his lips. Otherwise, his expression is unreadable. I peer into his dark orbs, searching for any sort of positive reaction to this news. But there's nothing, my not having a boyfriend seemingly as mundane a detail as how I take my coffee.

"So…" I tear my eyes away before I do or say something else I'll regret. Something else to make this awkward. "How's Grams doing?"

That's all it takes for a brilliant smile to light up his face, as I knew it would. I always admired the bond Asher had with his grandmother. "Still as headstrong and crazy as ever." A deep chuckle vibrates through his chest, natural and unforced. "She recently took up kickboxing, a fact I have first-hand knowledge of after witnessing it this past Christmas."

"You were in Florida?" I ask, recalling how his parents typically spent the colder months down south. His father's job as a financial planner allowed him to work from wherever he was. And spending November through April in the south allowed him to have clients in multiple parts of the country.

"Boston," he corrects. "Since Grams is getting older, Mom and Dad have been staying up north. Of course, she tries to insist she's fine, that age is only a number, and she has no intention of dying anytime soon."

"That sounds like something Grams would say." Regret squeezes at my heart, the heaviness settling deep in my chest.

Despite everything that transpired between Jessie and myself, I should have made more of an effort to stay in touch with Grams. She'd reached out to me in the months following the breakup, but I'd made my decision. The only way to repair the splintered fragments of my heart was to walk away from the entire family. It hurt too much otherwise. Which is why I should have walked out of that bar tonight when I had the chance. I fear it will take another eight years to repair my heart again.

"So... Kickboxing?" I press, swallowing back the memories.

"Right." He brightens his sympathetic gaze. "I'd been home for no more than five minutes when Grams walked in wearing workout clothes. And not, like, old granny workout clothes."

"Oh god." I cover my mouth with my hand. "Was she wearing spandex?"

He rubs his eyes. "I still have the image ingrained in my memory. I mean, she's in great shape for being nearly ninety, but still. After a while, gravity does its thing. Grams has never been one who cares what people think of her, though. Anyway, I'd barely had time to unpack when she came barreling in and said she was dragging me to her kickboxing class. Claimed she'd been telling all the people in her class about my music, that they were all dying to meet me. I thought about blowing her off, but she's getting older, so I indulged her. I figured we were going to the Y or the senior center. You can imagine my surprise when she directed me to the parking lot of some industrial building. It was an actual MMA gym."

I burst out laughing. As ridiculous as the picture he's painted sounds, it's entirely believable. Grams never adhered to society's expectations. And she certainly wouldn't let her age get in the way of doing something she wanted.

"What did you do?" I ask, wiping the corners of my eyes.

"What *could* I do? I'd be lying if I said I wasn't curious about the entire scenario. So I went in with her, prepared to defend her against any asshole who tried to tell her she should go somewhere else. But the second

30

she walked through those doors, everyone welcomed her. Hell, Grams even got into all the locker room talk, too. I will admit, she's got one hell of a round kick." He winces. "I found that out the hard way."

"How's that?"

"Let's just say I got a little too close and her leg hit me with such force that an ice pack was attached to my balls for the next twenty-four hours."

My laughter echoes in the restaurant, nostalgia filling me. Of all the people I lost when Jessie and I broke up, Grams was the hardest, more so than Jessie, or even Asher. She had this spirit, this vitality I felt drawn to the second I met her. Like she was a kindred spirit. Like she knew me and I her, even though she was a stranger to me at that point.

"Knowing Grams, she intentionally did that to prove she could take care of herself."

He lifts his coffee to his lips with a wink. "You're probably right."

"Here you go." Our waitress approaches, carrying two plates. "Red velvet pancakes." She sets the dish in front of me before turning toward Asher, her smile shifting from cordial to much more flirtatious. "And your steak and eggs." Her voice grows seductive as she places it in front of him, pushing her arms together to make her cleavage pop.

I take this opportunity to study her. Her appearance is similar to every other woman out here who's trying to catch their big break in modeling. Waif-thin. Blonde hair that's most likely not her natural color. Overdone makeup. Nothing about her stands out as remarkable. I'm not saying I'm supermodel material, but I hate the idea of Asher and this cookie-cutter blonde being together, as unlikely as that is. Or maybe it's the idea they *can* be together that irritates me. That she *can* flirt with him, and he her, with no consequences.

"Thank you. This looks delicious."

"Is there anything else I can get you?" Her voice becomes increasingly breathy. "Ketchup? Tabasco? More coffee? Or maybe something else?"

Asher waggles his brows at me before returning his attention to Waitress Barbie. "I believe I have everything I need right here." Eyes connecting with mine, he reaches across the table, grabbing my hand in his, gently brushing his thumb across my knuckles.

The subtle sensation causes me to inhale a sharp breath. I don't move. Don't blink. It's not the first time I've felt his hand on me. But this seems so much more charged than any of the other times he's touched me. Then again, that was *before*. When I was blind to everything and everyone other than Jessie York.

"Oh." Waitress Barbie straightens, her expression falling, but Asher doesn't seem to notice. If he does, he doesn't care, his stare still trained on me in a way that makes me think he's peeling back layer after layer, exposing every single one of my vulnerabilities. Or am I just imagining that, too?

One minute, I'm confident it's all in my head. The next, I feel something I didn't think possible, confident Asher does, too. This is why I've avoided dating for so long. It's too stressful.

"Well, if you change your mind, give me a shout."

She shoots her eyes to mine before spinning around. I'm about to pull my hand away, but Asher tightens his grasp.

I try not to read too much into it. We're just two friends holding hands. Hell, there were quite a few nights I'd dozed off on his shoulder as I listened to him strum his guitar at the lake house.

Each summer, I looked forward to spending time there. After dinner, we'd sit by the lake, a campfire burning, and actually talk to each other. No distractions. Spending time together in a way most people no longer do in this technology-driven society. Jessie would inevitably go inside early, complaining about the mosquitos, despite not having a single bite on his flesh. I should have known then we were incompatible. He hated everything to do with nature, preferring the pace of the city. While I love urban life, I enjoy getting away from it all, too. Something I haven't had the opportunity to do for too long now.

A squeeze on my hand brings me back from my memories, and I return my eyes to Asher as he releases his hold. "Sorry. I shouldn't have used you as a barrier, but I don't think she would have gotten the hint otherwise."

I smile weakly. "What are friends for?"

Chapter Four

"I CAN'T REMEMBER the last time I stayed out this late," I remark as Asher and I make our way across the nearly empty parking lot. It's now that in-between time of night. Most bar and clubgoers are passed out in their beds. The nine-to-fivers haven't started their day yet. The only people out and about are the insomniacs or the ones who seem to find inspiration in the romantic notion of being awake when the rest of the world sleeps. "Except the nights I work, but I don't consider that staying out late. It's not exactly voluntary, but something I do so I can pay my bills."

"I get it," he responds with a slight wink. "My body's hard-wired to stay up late, too. That was always the difficult part about teaching, and the part I don't miss. I could never adjust to the early hours. Grams always said it was because I inherited her non-conformist free spirit. It was hell waking up at six every morning after having gone to bed only a few hours earlier. Falling asleep by two was a good night."

I nod in understanding as we approach his car. He opens my door, and I slide into my seat. "That's why I don't mind working the night shift. I think it gives you a different perspective on things. Makes you see the world in a different light."

He ducks in behind the steering wheel, treating me to a small smile. "Glad to see there's still a little Holly Golightly in you."

I scrunch my brows.

"Holly Golightly," he repeats. "You know. *Breakfast at Tiffany's.*"

"I know who she is, but I—"

"The opening scene. When she's strolling down Fifth Avenue in an evening gown and stops in front of Tiffany's to eat her breakfast. Something about that scene always spoke to me. Like it was the calm before the storm. Few people get the opportunity to see Manhattan, or any city, so peaceful. I think that's why I do my best work at night after the world's gone to sleep. There's no distraction. No constant buzzing of my cell phone. I can lock myself away in the studio and write."

"Are you working on something now? A new album?"

"You could say that." He sucks his bottom lip between his teeth, glancing at me in contemplation. "Actually, it's something pretty big. Something that could change everything for me."

"That guy at the bar…," I begin, meeting Asher's gaze. "The one who said in a few months we wouldn't be able to turn on the radio without hearing your music."

"Wasn't lying," he states without me having to ask the question on the tip of my tongue. "As long as I meet this deadline. Honestly, I shouldn't have gone out tonight, but when Mark mentioned his band was in town, I figured taking a break and performing could be a good way to get the creative juices flowing again."

"Did it?"

He cranks the ignition, stealing a glance at me before reversing out of the parking spot. "I do believe it has."

He shifts into first and maneuvers the car through the lot, coming to a stop before merging onto the street. I focus on my surroundings, relishing in the chilly night air on my skin. The sky's no longer pitch-black as it was when we entered the restaurant. There's an almost purple-blue hue, a warning that daybreak is on the horizon.

We come to a stoplight, the lack of any noise unnerving, especially when I feel the heat of Asher's gaze on me. I glance his way, a flicker of something I can't explain in his expression. Yearning? Nostalgia perhaps? He parts his lips, peering at me as if my face holds the answer to whatever has him so conflicted.

Then his mouth quirks into a combination of a grin and a smirk. "Are you tired? Or do you think you can last a bit longer?"

A little voice in my brain warns me I've already spent more time with Asher than I should have. But just like those nights at Grams' lake house, I don't want tonight to end.

"Oh, baby, I can last all night long," I shoot back playfully. My smile falls quickly when I notice his grip on the steering wheel tighten. The vein in his neck throbs, his jaw ticks. I continue to stare, making sure I'm not imagining it. This time, I know I'm not. I see it. The quickening rise and fall of his chest. The constricting of his muscles. The flaring of his nostrils. All over what should have been a harmless sexual innuendo between friends, one I'd made several times with him in the past. But that was before. When it truly was harmless. I'm not sure I can say the same thing here.

Not saying a word, he pulls a quick U-turn, driving deeper into the night. The wind blows my hair as I observe the commercial buildings turn into more residential neighborhoods, the traffic becoming more and more sparse. I steal a glance into the rearview mirror to see the familiar silhouette of the Vegas Strip grow smaller and more distant behind me.

"Where are we going?" I break the cryptic silence.

"You'll see."

"So secretive."

"Trust me. If I told you, you wouldn't believe it. It's better if you see for yourself."

Desperate to cut through the stiff tension, I flash him a bright smile. "You've been moonlighting as an Elvis impersonator and have to perform a last-minute wedding for some celebrity A-listers."

He glances my way, his tight expression waning, his dimples popping. I remember looking through family photo albums from when Jessie and Asher were younger. Due to their proximity in age, it was often difficult to tell one from the other. Unless they were both smiling. Asher has these adorable dimples that have only made him more endearing with age. He can give off this tough, brooding persona of a tortured artist all he wants. But the second he smiles and those dimples pop, he looks like the boy next door.

Maybe the *bad* boy next door.

But he's not a bad boy, either. I'm not quite sure *how* to describe Asher York. I also wasn't sure back then.

"Nope. But good guess. Try again."

"Was I even remotely close?"

"The only thing I have in common with Elvis is that he could also play guitar and sing."

"Okay." I exhale dramatically, looking at the sky as I try to come up with yet another ridiculous scenario. When I return my eyes to Asher, I can't help but admire his carefree and relaxed demeanor. One hand rests on the steering wheel, the other on the gear shift. Something about how casual he is as he drives this beautiful classic car makes him appear even sexier than when he performs on stage.

"You have an audition for one of those all-male reviews and want me to give you a quick rundown from the striptease classes Bernadette made us attend a few days ago."

His wide eyes fling to mine, the vein in his neck pulsing once more. Maybe I shouldn't have mentioned those lessons.

"You took striptease classes?" His voice comes out as a low growl, heat and desire dripping from him. I can only imagine his reaction if I offered to give him a private show.

"And pole dance lessons."

"Fuck," he hisses, his hand sliding off the gear shift and onto my thigh, squeezing.

I remain still, unsure where to go from here. All I know is the way he's touching me has me wanting more, that spark returning with a vengeance.

He suddenly slams on the brakes, causing my body to jolt toward the windshield. The only things that keep me from crashing through it are the seatbelt and Asher's arm bracing me.

"Sorry." He clears his throat as he takes a quick left, the houses becoming more spread out and opulent. This isn't a regular residential neighborhood anymore. This is where the wealthy play when they're in Vegas. "Almost missed the turn."

"Did something distract you?" I tease.

"I'd have to surrender my man card if I *wasn't* distracted by that."

"I can see how that would be a problem with whoever sets the rules. Just like women are supposed to fawn over shirtless, well-built men as they dance on a stage, men are supposed to salivate over a woman on a pole."

"Not just any woman," he clarifies. "The idea of *you* pole dancing is, well… It's like every fantasy I've ever had." The flirtatious quality to his voice is gone, replaced with a truthfulness I didn't quite anticipate.

"Asher, I—"

"Here we are," he interrupts, his voice brightening. I study him for a moment, but his expression is even once again. Like he's flipped a switch, and any craving he exhibited mere seconds ago is nothing but a distant memory.

I look away, my brows drawing together when he pulls up to a gated driveway. He stops outside a box, inputting a four-digit code. The large, metal gates slowly open, granting us access.

"Who lives here?" I ask. "Do you have some wealthy benefactor, like Paul Varjak did in *Breakfast at Tiffany's*?"

He chuckles as he navigates up a winding driveway. The instant the sprawling mansion comes into view, my jaw drops. I have no idea what's going on, but my curiosity piques more and more with each beat of my heart.

"No wealthy benefactor. Well, not like that anyway. There's no rich older woman I'm sleeping with in order to bankroll my life while I write."

"Then—"

"Have you heard of Fallen Grace?"

I snort. "Who hasn't? You can't turn on the radio without hearing their music. Not to mention I work in pediatric oncology. I have several patients who are teenage girls. A few of them have even hung up posters of the band in their room."

Asher pulls the car into a detached garage off to the side of the main house and engages the parking brake, killing the ignition. I stare in awe at the row of sports cars. Tesla. Mercedes. BMW. Even a Maserati.

"They're patients long enough to decorate their rooms?" Asher's voice pulls me back from the myriad of questions swirling in my mind.

"Some of them will never walk out of that hospital again. Unless the family makes the decision to do home hospice care in their final days."

"But they're kids." He shakes his head, heartache etched in the lines of his face over this sad truth I confront daily.

"Cancer doesn't discriminate. Young. Old. Rich. Poor. It doesn't matter."

He stares deeper into my eyes. Then he reaches toward me, cupping my cheek, his long fingers burrowing into my thick hair. "You are an incredible woman, Izzy. I've never met anyone as compassionate and selfless as you. You deserve better than…" He trails off, stopping himself from finishing his sentence. He doesn't need to. I know what he was about to say. "Well, you deserve better."

"Thank you."

He keeps his hand on my cheek a heartbeat longer. For a second, I think he's about to kiss me, the way his gaze strays to my mouth and he licks his own lips in preparation. Kissing him would be wrong, would violate the unspoken rule against falling for a woman your friend — your *brother* — already dated. But it doesn't bother me like it should.

He closes his eyes and I tilt my head toward him, my breathing increasing in anticipation. Then his shoulders fall and he drops his hold on me, his expression pinched, as if reminding himself of who we are. Who we'll always be to one another.

"Come on." With shaky hands, he opens the door and steps out of the car, rushing around to help me. A stiff silence fills the air as he leads me out of the garage and down a path lined with succulents in a stone bed.

I glance up at the vast, two-story house that would rival some of the ones I grew up near in Greenwich, still having no answers about who lives in it and what we're doing here, other than it having to do with one of the most popular boy bands around today.

"Is this Fallen Grace's party house?" Chloe had mentioned several celebrities owned houses on the outskirts of the city for that exact purpose. Since she works as a celebrity news columnist, she would know.

"They bought it for that purpose a few years ago, but lately it has served as more of a recording studio."

I halt in my tracks, mouth agape, eyes wide. I didn't expect him to agree with my statement. "This is Fallen Grace's party house-slash-recording studio?"

He shrugs, as if he'd just told me he had to do laundry or some other mundane task. "Sure is."

I blink, gawking at him. Then the house. Then back at him. "Are they here? Am I going to meet Fallen Grace? Some of my teenage patients would lose their minds, especially if I'm able to get their autographs."

"They're home in London for a break before we hit it hard in a few weeks."

"We?"

His grin widens as he extends his hand toward me. "Come on. I'll explain everything."

I stare at his hand with skepticism before lifting my eyes to his. He arches a brow, tilting his head slightly. I wonder if this is how Alice felt when she noticed the White Rabbit scurrying past her. If she was torn between remaining in her normal life and experiencing something she'd never forget, even if it was fleeting. But that didn't stop her from following the White Rabbit. I don't let it stop me, either.

Blowing out a breath, I place my hand in his, following him deeper and deeper down my own rabbit hole.

But there's no place I'd rather be.

Chapter Five

"**Y**OU LIVE HERE now?" I ask as I run my fingers along the cool ivory of a baby grand piano, floating my eyes to where Asher leans against the soundproof wall in a state-of-the-art recording studio. No more walls and ceiling covered with egg crate foam to prevent outside noise from filtering into the basement of his parents' house. This is all professionally constructed and designed. A musician's dream.

"It's more a temporary home out of convenience. The guys need to get a new album out, as well as prepare for an extended engagement at one of the casinos. I need to be somewhere I have access to whatever I require. Granted, when they first approached me to help with the new album, the plan *was* to record in LA."

I sit on the piano bench, lightly pressing the keys, the soft sound filling the room. It's been years since I've played, but it's like riding a bike. You may have a few slips and falls at first, but once muscle memory kicks in, you're cruising right along.

"And how *did* they approach you?"

"Pure dumb luck." He pushes off the wall and closes in on me in three long strides, sitting next to me. "Or maybe the big man upstairs decided to give me a break." He places his hands on the piano keys, playing a simple baseline to compliment the B-flat blues progression I'm fooling around with. "To be honest, I was ready to give up. I was months behind on rent and facing eviction."

"Was gigging your only source of income?" I play with a little more confidence, my transitions coming with greater ease.

"I taught private guitar and piano lessons in the afternoons, so that helped," he answers, looking at me instead of the keys. He could probably play it blindfolded.

Mmm... Asher in a blindfold.

I extinguish the thought, silently berating my libido for going there.

"I had enough money in savings to keep me afloat for a little while. But after a year, that savings had dwindled to practically nothing. I'd reached the point where I didn't see any other option but to go back home, tell my parents they were right and it was a crazy idea, then hope they'd let me move in with them while I got my master's degree so I could teach again."

"That sucks," I respond, hitting the wrong note, causing a dissonance. I cringe, but Asher smiles, shrugging it off. I'm sure he's heard much worse musicians than myself. Hell, he used to teach beginner strings. If there's any class requiring earplugs and sedatives, it's that one.

"So one day, my phone in my hand, about to call Mom to ask if she'd help me settle up my affairs in LA so I could leave this chapter of my life behind, it rang with a number I didn't recognize. I almost didn't answer. Figured it was another bill collector."

"But you did."

"I did." He sighs, his posture relaxing, his lips kicking up into a small smile. It's obvious how grateful he is for this opportunity, that he has no intention of taking it for granted. "And that was the phone call that changed my life. Changed everything. I was seconds away from quitting, Iz. *Seconds*," he emphasizes, his voice brimming with passion and intensity, the music he's playing matching it.

I steal a glance at the way his fingers move across the delicate ivory with ease. I could watch him play for hours and never tire of it. It's so hypnotizing. So captivating. So mesmerizing.

"I truly believe some bigger force intervened, saying 'not yet'. At first, I thought it was a prank."

"Why's that?"

"Think about it. If you were a struggling musician, months behind on your rent and living off Ramen noodles, something you never even had to do in college, how would you respond to getting a phone call from someone purporting to be the manager of one of the highest grossing musical acts of the past decade, offering you a job writing and producing their new album?"

I smile. "I'd think it was a joke, too."

"David, their manager, knew it would probably come as a surprise. He convinced me to meet him the following morning and judge for myself. When I walked into the luxurious office in Century City, I knew it wasn't a prank. Gold and platinum records hung on the wall. Posh furniture filled the space. Hell, I'm pretty sure even the receptionist's shoes cost more than my rent. Christian Lou-something."

"Louboutins," I interject. "They're Christian Louboutins. They have this signature red sole that all women foam at the mouth over."

He cocks a brow. "Including you?"

I pinch my lips together as I focus on the white and black keys in front of me, the melody coming easier now, even if I am sticking close to the chord progressions. Unlike Asher, who's riffing off the tune as if it's second nature to improvise a song on the spot.

"A girl can dream, can't she?" While I'm not one to spend a fortune on clothes or shoes, considering I spend most of my life wearing scrubs, I can still look. Can still pine. Can still fantasize.

A pair of Christian Louboutins is the female equivalent of a wet dream coming true.

"She certainly can."

"So, what happened next?"

"I was brought into this incredible corner office that was bigger than my entire apartment, the five members of Fallen Grace sitting on the two couches. If I hadn't gotten that phone call the previous night, I probably wouldn't have recognized them, but I did some research. I'd *heard* of Fallen Grace, but I'm not exactly a pre-pubescent girl, so I didn't know what they looked like."

"I could probably tell you which one has dimples, which one has the goatee, and which one has the 'adorable' birthmark right above his lip," I retort sarcastically. "They're just so *dreamy*." I bat my lashes, mimicking the way some of my patients fawn over their teen idols.

He chuckles. "Well, I couldn't. I'd never even listened to their music until I got that phone call. After doing so, I wasn't sure why they called me. Or how they even found me. My stuff isn't the pop music they typically perform."

"Right. So…"

"When I asked about it, their manager told me they were tired of the normal 'dog and pony show', as they called it. Wanted to go for a different, more mature sound now that they were in their mid-twenties. If they didn't want to die the same death every other boy band seemed to, they needed to do something to make themselves attractive to a broader audience."

"Take the 'boy' out of boy band," I offer.

"Exactly. They'd brought in some of the top songwriters to help with the transition, but no one 'got it'. They were all professionals who'd made a living writing melodies and lyrics that were popular. The band already knew what was popular. They didn't want that anymore. So they started hanging out in area bars in various cities, checking out the local music scene. Incognito, of course."

"And they just so happened to be at a bar in LA where you were performing?" I tilt my head at him, then quickly return my attention to the piano when I hit another wrong note. After looking at Asher's fingers to figure out where we were in the progression, I recenter my hands on an F-major-seven chord, regaining my confidence.

"They were. Well, one of them was anyway. Grabbed a postcard I was giving out containing free download codes of the songs I'd written. Played it for the rest of the guys, then their manager. And the rest, as they say, is history."

"So you're actually writing the songs for Fallen Grace's new album?" It seems so far-fetched, like something he'd tell a girl in a bar to get her to sleep with him.

"I am."

My fingers fall from the piano as it sinks in. Why didn't he mention anything earlier? Maybe he couldn't. Maybe he's under a non-disclosure agreement. That would make sense, considering the band probably hasn't gone public with this new direction yet.

"The way you made it sound, you were only here for the weekend."

"I never said anything like that." He shrugs. "You assumed."

"But you still didn't correct my assumption when it was obvious what I was thinking, especially when I asked how long it takes to get here from LA. Why?"

The music fades away as he stops playing, facing me. "I guess I wanted to make sure you were the same Isabella I remember. That you'd want to spend time with me for me. Not because of all this." He waves a hand around. Guitars of every brand hanging along the wall. A drum kit sitting in the corner that any serious drummer would drool over. Even a wet bar with top-shelf liquor so you don't have to venture into the house for a drink.

Resting my hand on his arm, I lock eyes with him, refusing to look at anything else. "I've always enjoyed spending time with you for you, Asher. Everything else has always just been…noise."

A tiny exhale of air escapes his lips as they part, a slow smile building. He scoops my hand off his arm, holding it in his, running his thumb along my skin. This time, he doesn't have an overly amorous waitress as an excuse for touching me. He doesn't have any excuse, other than he wants to, *needs* to. I try to tell myself it's a platonic gesture between two old friends, but the tenderness with which he brushes my knuckles, the darkening of his eyes, tell me that's not the case. Tell me we could very well be playing with fire.

An outside force pulls me toward him, a tether keeping our bodies bound to each other. As I lean closer, Asher shifts his eyes to my lips. His shoulders rise and fall in a quicker pattern, his grip on my hand tightening to the point of being nearly painful. A tumultuous tug-of-war plagues his expression. Desire, then guilt. Infatuation, then indifference. Hunger, then repulsion.

His conscience winning out, he jumps up from the bench, stalking toward the door. "It's almost sunrise." His voice trembles with the aftereffects of his internal battle.

I can't even pretend to be surprised by his abrupt retreat. That seems to be the game we're playing. One step forward. A giant leap backward. A promise to move ahead. Then a swift change of course. Or maybe change of heart.

"It's beautiful off the back patio. You should really see it. It'll be like old times."

I sigh, briefly closing my eyes before standing. "Like old times," I repeat, meeting him in the doorway.

He offers me an apologetic smile, which I return with a nod of understanding. Then he leads me out of the recording studio and down the long corridor lined with framed prints of some of the biggest names in the industry. When we emerge into the living area, he continues toward a set of French doors, opening one and allowing me to step outside before him.

"This way." He rests his hand on my lower back, steering me through a luxurious patio, complete with a fire pit, past what appears to be a regulation pool, and up to the edge of the property. A glow has already begun to sneak out behind the mountains in the distance.

I'd always thought Las Vegas to be flat. For the most part, it is, but this house sits on a parcel of land that's elevated enough so I can see the Strip with no obstruction.

"Not my favorite city in the world, but it's home to one hell of a sunrise."

"Even better than at the lake house?"

49

A smile radiates through his features. "Well, I wouldn't go that far." He rests his forearms on the steel fence surrounding the property, peering into the distance, deep in thought. I do the same, basking in what I know will be our last few minutes together. We've settled into our old routine. A few drinks. A bite to eat, although it used to be in the form of roasting marshmallows and hotdogs. Playing music. Watching the sunrise. Then going our separate ways.

"I hope it's not too bold of me to say…" He leans toward me, "but the reason I loved those sunrises was because of *who* I often had the pleasure of watching them with." The heat of his breath on my neck sends an involuntary tremble racing through me.

"Are you cold?" he asks, oblivious to the fact that my reaction was because of him. Because of his words. His honesty. His everything. "Let me grab a sweatshirt for you." He starts toward the house, but I wrap my hand around his bicep, stopping him.

"Don't." I quickly release my hold on him, increasing the space between us before I'll no longer be able to control myself. "I wouldn't want you to miss the sunrise."

I resume my position, subconsciously rubbing my arms to fight against the chill as I watch the glow make its gradual ascent over the peaks. It's unlike any sunrise I've seen. One side of the mountain is in light. The other still shrouded in relative darkness. Like an eclipse.

As I marvel at how beautiful this planet truly is, a presence approaches from behind. Asher wraps me in his embrace, pulling me into his strong body.

"Glad to see some things never change," he comments, running his calloused hands up and down my arms.

"What do you mean by that?"

"You're still as stubborn as you were all those years ago. When we sat and watched the sunrise together at the lake, you never let me run inside to grab you a sweatshirt. Why's that?"

I'm not sure what comes over me. Maybe it's the lack of sleep. Maybe it's feeling like this is a dream. Or maybe it's the idea that I've longed to be in this man's presence again for the past eight years. So instead of brushing off his question, I do something I normally wouldn't. I offer him a piece of the truth, regardless of how he'll respond. In a few hours, I'll be on a plane heading back to my life, and he'll return to his. May as well take a risk.

"I didn't want to lose the moment," I answer in a soft voice. "Didn't want it to disappear."

I don't have to turn around to feel the smile on his lips. He draws me closer, the sear of his breath on my nape spreading a glow within. "I won't disappear."

"Here we are," Asher announces as he pulls the car into the valet area under the awning leading to the lobby.

"Here we are," I repeat, pretending not to be as forlorn over the idea of saying goodbye as I am. The entire drive here, I wanted to tell him to take me back so we could have another day, another hour, another minute. But it's after seven in the morning. Chloe and I are supposed to leave for the airport at eleven. That only gives me a few hours to get a little sleep so I'm not a complete zombie.

But I'd gladly trade those few hours of sleep for more time with Asher. To recreate whatever I experienced the last several hours.

He holds my gaze, his expression making me think there's a question on the tip of his tongue. As seemed to be the case all night, he shakes it off, stepping out of the car and making his way around to my side, helping me to my feet.

"Promise you'll stay in touch." He brushes that same errant strand of hair behind my ear. "That you won't shut me out because—"

"I promise," I respond, saving him from having to bring up Jessie.

"Good."

I shift on my feet, uncertain of the protocol in saying goodbye to your ex-fiancé's brother, whom you fantasized about kissing on more than one occasion throughout the night. I doubt there is one.

"Well then…" I clear my throat, stepping back. "It was—"

Before I can utter another syllable, he advances and clutches my face in his hands. It steals my breath, a current pulsating through me. I swallow hard as I'm forced to stare into the fervor in his deep-set eyes, years' worth of longing swirling into a tidal pool of lust.

"Izzy." The way my name rolls off his tongue has my insides coiling and tightening. It's husky, yet still prayer-like. A wanton benediction. A sensual communion.

My virtuous sin.

His lips inch closer and closer as his grasp on my face becomes harsher, more punishing, more consuming. I can physically feel the battle waging, his mouth struggling to advance while the wounded pieces of him sound a retreat, yanking him back.

His chest heaves, muscles shaking, everything about this moment so surreal, so hypnotizing, so fucking perfect. I don't even care if he actually kisses me or not. The knowledge he *wants* to is enough.

With a growl, he tears his hands from me, anguish and turmoil covering his expression. A beat passes, then another as he hangs his head, attempting to collect himself. When he returns his eyes to mine, they're no longer inflamed, those of an untamed beast. They're even, albeit still flickering with want.

He expels a sigh and brushes his lips against my forehead. The touch is slight, yet profound. More profound than any act of intimacy I've experienced these last few years. Because with just the most subtle of touches, I feel the meaning behind it.

"Thanks for tonight. It was exactly what I needed."

"Me, too," I respond with a half-hearted smile when he pulls back.

"Go get some rest."

"You, too."

"I don't think I could sleep if I tried," he admits.

"No?"

He treats me to one last devilish grin, slowly shaking his head. "No. Can't waste this."

"Waste what?"

He grabs my hand in his, bringing my knuckles up to his lips. His eyes remain glued to mine as he feathers a soft kiss across the skin.

"You inspire me." He allows his words to linger in the air between us. Then he drops his hold on me, rushing to his car and jumping behind the wheel. He cranks the ignition, which roars to life, grabbing the attention of a few valet attendants and early-morning stragglers making their way to whatever hotel they're staying at.

As he's about to drive off, he glances back at me. "You've *always* inspired me."

Chapter Six

I STARE OUT the windows of the airline lounge, watching airplanes prepare to depart. I've always found airports fascinating. It probably comes from my mother's background as a flight attendant and her love of flying, but something about air travel speaks to the romantic in me, even if it's nowhere as glamorous as it once was.

"Thank God for espresso." Chloe's voice cuts through my moment of peace. I shift my eyes forward as she plops onto the chair across from me. "It's good for what ails you. Like I always say…"

"I know, I know. When you need something stronger than coffee but weaker than cocaine."

"Precisely. So, back to work tomorrow?" She avoids my eyes, looking out at the runway.

"Don't think you're getting out of this so easily," I warn, then lean toward her, lowering my voice. "Who was that guy I saw you practically humping in the lobby?"

"Humping? Did you just say humping?"

I take a sip of my coffee, needing it to keep my eyelids open. Thankfully, my body has learned to function on minimal sleep so the few hours I had once I returned to my room is enough to trick my body into thinking it got more.

"You're deflecting. Just like you did the entire ride to the airport."

"Which lasted all of ten minutes."

"Still…" I raise my brows in expectation, a silent warning I have no intention of dropping the subject until she talks.

When I walked into the lobby to meet Chloe earlier, I was convinced my eyes were deceiving me. Or there was a Chloe doppelgänger roaming the streets of Vegas. The last thing I expected to encounter was my friend, who's always shunned any semblance of romance, wrapped in a man's embrace, about to kiss him. Until a group of rowdy guys, who didn't look old enough to drink, bumped into her, making her lose her balance. We'd been in Vegas for four days and she never mentioned meeting a guy. Based on the way he looked at her, this was not their first encounter.

Then again, I haven't told her about running into Asher. I'm not prepared for the barrage of questions she'll inevitably have. I'm still uncertain how to answer my own, especially after his admission that I've always inspired him.

"You can't avoid this forever. We do have a five-hour flight where I can continue to pester you until you tell me what I want to know. And I can be *very* annoying. You should know that by now."

Her mouth in a tight line, she studies me for a few moments, then sighs. "Fine." Uncrossing her arms, she brings her espresso back to her lips, taking a sip. "Remember the club we went to our first night here?"

I roll my eyes. "I'd rather forget it."

"Wouldn't we all." She mirrors my own sentiments on the ridiculousness of this weekend.

"So…" I arch an expectant brow.

"Remember when I excused myself to get a drink after Bernadette demanded blow job shots at the top of her lungs?"

I nod.

"Well, after I got my drink and was on my way back, some guy came up to me thinking I was a prostitute. I tried to tell him I wasn't, but I'm pretty sure he was dropped on his head too many times as a child because he refused to believe me."

"So… What? You see him in the lobby this morning and decide to kiss him?"

She scrunches up her face. "God no. If I ever run into him again, I'll knee him in the balls, like I should have the other night. But before I had the chance, an arm wrapped around me and pried me out of his grasp."

"An arm?" I give her a sideways glance.

A smile unlike any I've seen on my friend's face pulls on her mouth, serenity engulfing her. "A really muscular and defined arm dressed in a blazer." She stares into the distance for another beat before returning her eyes to mine. "He ended up sending the guy packing with his balls between his legs. Then I thought *he* was trying to pick me up because he called me 'Dick Girl'. In reality, he was calling me that because of the stupid penis necklace Bernadette insisted we all wear."

"I didn't think you were gone *that* long."

"I wasn't."

"Apparently long enough for him to leave an impression on you."

"That, and we kept bumping into each other all weekend. The other night, I went to the Italian restaurant off the casino floor to get something to eat before the striptease and pole dance classes. He was there. Sat next to me. Had this incredibly sensual conversation. Paid for my tab. Then this morning, as I was riding down to the lobby, the elevator stopped on the floor below mine. Wouldn't you know it? When the doors opened, he stood there, waiting to get on. So we walked to the lobby together, then he left."

"But—"

"He came back. Said he couldn't leave without kissing me." Her mouth crawls into a dreamy smile again, a blush blooming on her cheeks as she seems to glow from the memory.

I can't remember the last time Chloe has talked about a guy like this. Hell, I can't remember the last time she's talked about a guy…period. She has her reasons, the most prominent being an alcoholic mother she's been taking care of the past decade. She doesn't think she can manage both.

"And, considering you saw the rest, that brings you up to speed."

"So… Who is he?"

She sips her espresso. "Like I told you earlier, just some guy."

"His name would suffice."

She shrugs. "I don't know it."

My jaw slackens and I lean toward her. "You mean to tell me that, of the three times you've seen him—"

"Four, if you count him coming back to try to kiss me."

"Whatever…" I wave her off. "That's not the point. The point is that you never thought to ask him his name?"

"I *did* think of it."

"A name is usually the *first* thing I ask. You'd think with all the time you spent 'bumping' into each other this weekend, you would have gotten that much."

"It's just…" She exhales, visibly flustered. I want to ask who this imposter is and what she's done with my friend. The woman who doesn't let anyone or anything get to her. "Every time I saw him…" Her expression softens as she shakes her head, her tone contemplative. Her eyes shine with weightlessness. "It was quiet."

"Quiet? What do you mean?"

Setting her small cup on the coffee table between us, she angles toward me. "All the noise of my life…" Her voice is no louder than a whisper, as if worried someone she knows might overhear and announce to the world that underneath the hard outer shell is someone who wants the same thing we all do. "It was…gone."

I nod. Although Chloe and I aren't as close as we once were, there's something to be said about being around when the shit hits the fan, so to speak. And I was there when the shit hit the fan in Chloe's life. When her parents divorced. When she left the quaint, upper middle-class neighborhood in Connecticut and started a new life in New Jersey with her mother. When she tried to hide the fact that her mother was an alcoholic.

But I knew.

Chloe can hide from a lot of people. But she can't hide from me. I see through it all. Even the shit she doesn't think anyone knows.

"Sometimes you just need someone to quiet it for a minute," I respond thoughtfully, giving her a reassuring smile.

"Because of that, I didn't think a name was necessary."

Our eyes lock, my expression relaying complete understanding. Then her lips turn into a devious grin. "You *do* have to admit, the entire scenario is kind of hot. Not knowing his name, anything about him…"

"*Kind of* hot?" I giggle, fanning myself. "Try off the charts! I noticed the chemistry between you two right away, even if all he did was kiss your cheek. It was incredibly…sexy. I can't imagine how it made *you* feel."

"Like I could let go. For once, I didn't worry about the fact that we're polar opposites. That he's presumably this guy who has his shit together, whereas I'm lucky if I don't lock myself out of my apartment on a daily basis. But each time I saw him, I didn't think about any of that, didn't try to distance myself because of how it would play out. It's almost like we were in our own little bubble."

"Bubbles can be good," I respond, knowing all too well what she's going through. I felt the same way with Asher all evening. Like we were protected from the reality of who we were to each other, even if for a brief moment. "Especially a bubble that sexy." My voice brightens, and I hope Chloe can't see past *my* walls as easily as I can peer through hers.

She stares at me for a split second with her analytical eyes. I hold my breath, waiting for her to pounce. Then she breaks into a laugh, and I follow, sending up a silent prayer. I'm not sure how I'll ever be able to explain my night with Asher to anyone. I'm not sure I want to. I want to keep that memory mine. Hold it close and cherish it once I return to New York.

"So, what do you think the girls are up to today?" she asks once our laughter dies down.

"Knowing Bernadette, something cliché and inappropriate."

"If I ever get that lonely and desperate for attention, promise me you'll smack some sense into me and tell me I don't need to stay in a loveless marriage. That there's better out there for me."

"You know I will," I assure her just as a chiming echoes from her cell phone.

She glances to where it sits on the table, and I steal a peek, seeing her mother's name appear on the screen.

With haste, she grabs the phone, firing off a quick text before placing it back down.

"She doing okay?" I ask, a touch of hesitation in my voice.

"Yeah." She reaches for her espresso, finishing it. "She's been dating this guy who works in the same building." She looks past me, a smile pulling on her lips. So uncharacteristic. "It's actually a sweet story. Somehow, they kept riding up to their floors in the same elevator. After about a week, he mentioned it to her. Said he couldn't ignore it anymore, that it was a sign."

"Hmm… A sign?" My lips quirk up.

"That's *not* the same thing," she snips back, fully aware I'm referring to her multiple encounters with her mystery man this weekend.

The same could be said about my chance encounter with Asher. Maybe it was a sign that I shouldn't have erased him from my life. But it's harder to call one random meeting a sign.

"Mom works in the same building as Aaron. There's a decent likelihood of running into him again. This thing with me and…whoever he is, well… It's different. I have a better chance of winning the lottery than seeing him again."

"You're probably right, but what if you do?"

"It'll never happen," she retorts. "I'm about to get on a flight back to New York. He was headed…" She waves her hand around, "wherever. So yeah. Not going to happen."

"But if it does?" I press, this time more out of curiosity. A part of me wants…*needs* to hear Chloe admit that maybe she'll consider pursuing something, despite all the obstacles in her life, even if many of them are self-imposed. Then I won't feel so mixed up about

Asher. The way his fingers warmed my skin. The way his body felt against mine. The way his words filled me with hope.

"It won't," she insists.

"But if it does?"

"It won't."

"Yeah, but if it does?"

She groans, dramatically rolling her eyes. "Fine. If by some miracle I *do* see him again, maybe I'll admit there might be a reason for it all."

I nod, leaning back into my chair, content with her answer.

"But it won't happen," she adds.

I glare at her. "Always have to have the last word, don't you?"

"Always."

Her phone dings once more, probably another text from her mother, and she grabs it. "Shit," she mutters as my own phone chimes.

"What is it?" I reach into my bag, retrieving my cell. A part of me hopes it's a text from Asher. Instead, it's an alert from the airline. "Dammit."

"Yup. Flight to JFK is canceled."

I close my eyes, pinching the bridge of my nose. "Just how I want to spend my day. Stuck in the airport." Normally, a canceled flight wouldn't bother me. But I was looking forward to getting on that plane and catching up on my sleep. I hate the idea of sitting in this hellhole all day while we wait for another flight.

"And not any airport." She gestures in the direction of the terminal, past the doors of the serene lounge, the clanging of slot machines faint but still ever present. I have a feeling I'm going to hear that noise for the next few weeks. "McCarran Airport in *fabulous* Las Vegas. If

61

the Strip is the tenth circle of hell, this place is purgatory."

"Glad to see all those literature classes paid off."

"What flight did they rebook you on?" She looks at her phone, and I do the same.

"Red-eye. Eleven PM. And here's the kicker. No seat assignment available." I hold out my cell toward her.

"Me, too."

"It looks like they're cramming everyone onto that flight. What are the chances of us actually getting on?" I ask rhetorically.

"I'd like to say they wouldn't rebook us just to tell us no in ten hours."

"My mother used to work for an airline," I remind her. "They absolutely *would* do such a thing. I'll be right back."

Without giving her a chance to ask what I'm up to, I jump from my chair and walk with determined strides toward the front desk of the lounge, where it appears several other people on the same flight are attempting to rebook.

As I wait, I come up with a plan. If we're able to get seats, I'll take that as a sign I'm supposed to leave my one night with Asher as just that — one night. But if we can't, maybe it's the universe's way of saying we weren't supposed to have left things the way we did. That we're supposed to explore what I'm confident he felt, too. The connection. The electricity. The passion. God, I've missed having this kind of passion in my life.

When it's my turn, the agent waves me over with a smile. "Let me guess. You're on the canceled flight to JFK."

"Yes. Both my friend and I were rebooked on the red-eye tonight without any seat assignment. What are the chances we'll actually get on that flight?"

"I'm sure—"

"I know how these things work," I interrupt. "My mother is a former airline employee. We suffered through all those standby employee trips for years. And I'd rather not have to do that again. So just tell me how far down the list we are. Unless you can get us seats now."

Blowing out a sigh, she taps at her keyboard for a moment. "What's your name?"

"Isabella Nolan. And my friend is Chloe Davenport."

She refocuses on the screen, a slight cringe crossing her expression. "It's oversold," she tells me, although I already knew that. "Doesn't mean you *won't* get on."

"But we're pretty far down on the request list, right?"

"Since you're a displaced traveler, you do have priority."

"But there's an entire flight of displaced travelers," I argue back.

"I can get you confirmed seats on the noon flight to JFK tomorrow if you'd prefer."

"Let me go check with my friend. I'll be right back."

"Certainly."

I spin around, hurrying back to tell Chloe the news. "I can get us guaranteed seats on the noon flight tomorrow. The red-eye is oversold and they'll most likely be forced to rebook again if they can't get enough people with confirmed seats to give them up. You in? Guaranteed seats or take a risk on the red-eye?"

She blows out a breath, rubbing her temples. It's more than apparent she's not too keen about being stuck in this town. Maybe I should have pushed harder to get us on the red-eye. But the truth remains. The instant I saw our flight was canceled, hope brimmed inside me. Grams always said, "*With every new day we're given a new chance."* Maybe this is my new chance. For what? I'm not quite sure, but I can't shake the feeling there's a bigger reason for this.

"Guaranteed seats."

I brim with excitement, but do my best to hide it. "Give me your boarding pass and I'll get you rebooked." I hold out my hand. She places her phone into it, her boarding pass on the screen. "Thanks. Be right back."

I return to the desk and approach the same agent, handing her both our boarding passes. Within a few moments, we're rebooked. As I turn to head back to Chloe, my phone dings. I figure it's just my new flight information, but glance at the screen anyway. When I see Asher's name, my heart ricochets into my throat. Speaking of signs…

> *Safe travels today. Seeing you again was the highlight of my month. Hell, probably my year. I hope our paths cross again soon.*

I chew on my bottom lip as I read his text. I may regret what I'm about to do, may be trying to see something that's not there, but some other force is pulling the strings.

Drawing in a deep breath, I find Asher's contact in my phone and press it, listening to it ring.

"Izzy?" he answers almost immediately. All these years later and he still has the same number. Then again, so do I.

"Hey, Ash."

"Is everything okay?"

"I suppose…," I respond in a drawn-out voice before blurting, "My flight was canceled. Chloe and I are stuck in Vegas for another night. And—"

"Do you need a place to stay?" he offers without a moment's hesitation. "You're both more than welcome to come here."

"Are you sure? I wouldn't want to put you out. I know you're trying to write."

"An old college buddy is visiting today, so I won't get much writing done anyway." He lowers his voice. "And I'd love to have more time with you. I hated leaving you this morning with the thought that another eight years would go by without seeing you. Now I get one more chance."

A shiver rolls through me at the huskiness in his tone. I try to tell myself he doesn't mean anything by it, that his words don't carry the double meaning my sex-starved brain attributes to them. He's an old friend. Nothing more.

"We'll be there in about an hour," I say, not responding to his comment. "Maybe sooner. Is that okay?"

"Absolutely. I'll text you the address and gate code. Come on up once you get here."

"Sounds good."

"Perfect."

I stay on the line, almost waiting for him to back out, tell me this isn't a good idea. After the constant see-saw last night, it's not out of the realm of possibilities. But he doesn't.

"See you soon, Iz."

"See you soon, Ash."

I go to disconnect when he calls my name. "Izzy?"

"Yes?"

"I'm really glad your flight was canceled."

I exhale a tiny breath. "Me, too."

Chapter Seven

QUEASINESS SETTLES DEEP in my stomach as our Uber makes the turn onto Asher's street. My eyes are laser-focused out the window, avoiding Chloe's inquisitive stare crawling along my skin from across the back seat of the car. She hasn't pressed about this so-called "friend I knew in college" who we'd be crashing with. Now that we're driving past large estates that rival the size of those on all those celebrity lifestyle shows, I can sense her curiosity grow. I don't have to look at her to know her eyes are wide, her mouth agape, her brows pinched. It's how *I* looked a few hours ago.

"Right here," I tell the driver when I see the familiar gate come into view. He slows to a stop in front of the sprawling house, and I inhale a calming breath. This isn't a ludicrous idea, is it? God, I hope not. Only time will tell.

"Where the hell are we? David Copperfield's house?" Chloe quips.

"No." I make a show of collecting my purse and laptop bag. "But my sources say he lives around here somewhere."

"Sources? What sources? *I'm* your source for all things celebrity."

"Maybe there are some things about me you *don't* know."

More than she realizes.

66

My fingers on the handle, I pass her a conniving smile, then climb onto the sidewalk. It's strange not to be met with a barrage of cars or slot machines, as would have happened had we stayed at a hotel on the Strip. How does that saying go? *"Toto, I don't think we're in Kansas anymore."* Well, we're certainly not in the Las Vegas Chloe was probably expecting. We've flown over the rainbow. At least I have.

I walk toward the trunk where our driver is retrieving our bags. When Chloe doesn't immediately appear, I head to her side, rapping on the window before opening the door.

"Are you coming? Or do you want to call Bernadette and see if you can crash with her tonight? Maybe stay up and do a makeover, then go to some Pure Romance party."

"I wouldn't mind going to a Pure Romance party." She scoots out of the car. "I'm all for women exploring their sexuality. But I'll pass on the Bernadette makeover. With the amount of makeup she'd cake on my face and the revealing outfit she'd stuff me in, I'd come out of there looking like a blowup doll." Collecting her bag from our driver, she smiles her thanks, then walks up to the gate with me.

I retrieve my phone to verify the code Asher texted earlier and punch it into the security box. Once the gate slides open, I continue up the elaborate driveway. When I don't sense Chloe following, I glance over my shoulder.

"Are you coming?" I huff once more, this time with irritation for good measure.

"I suppose…" She continues toward me with reluctant steps, neither one of us saying a word as she takes in the well-maintained grounds that make it appear as if a gardener comes daily.

But the second we round the corner and Chloe is treated to her first glimpse of the house, that silence comes to an end. As I knew it would. I'm not stupid enough to think I wouldn't have to tell her this "friend" is Asher York. I didn't want her to talk me out of this, to remind me of all the reasons this is a bad idea. I have enough of those on my own without her adding to them.

"Iz?" she says as we approach the front steps.

I face her, albeit with reservation.

"Who lives here?"

"Just an old friend from my undergrad days."

"A…friend? Does this 'friend' happen to be of the male persuasion?"

"Yes." I straighten my spine, but still don't look her directly in the eyes.

"Call me crazy——"

"You certainly are."

"But I get the feeling there's more to the story than this guy being just a 'friend'."

I worry my bottom lip. How do I explain I spent all night with my ex-fiancé's brother without her throwing a yellow flag on the play?

I can insist we're only friends, that we ran into each other last night and caught up, which *is* the truth. If I'd run into anyone else from my college days, that would be the story I'd tell. But I felt it the first time I saw Asher perform, before I'd even heard the name Jessie York. I felt it last night when I heard his voice after so many years. And I felt it this morning when we said what I thought would be goodbye to each other.

Asher will always be something more than simply a friend. He will always own a piece of my heart.

"What is it?" She rests her hand on my bicep, giving me a reassuring smile. "You can tell me anything."

68

"I know that. But this..." I shake my head, staring into the distance, as if the answer is there. I doubt there will ever be a solution to this jumbled puzzle I've trapped myself in by accepting Asher's invitation to stay at his house for the night. Drawing in a deep breath, I bring my eyes back to hers. "It's Asher York."

Everything seems to stop now that the truth is out there. Time. The earth's rotation. Hell, even the birds have grown silent, the breeze gone, everything still in the stagnant desert air.

"Asher York? As in Jessie York's older brother?" she asks calmly, her expression unreadable, which only heightens my edginess.

"It's not exactly a common name, is it?" I laugh, trying to cover my nerves, but it has the opposite effect.

"Asher York, the handsome, struggling musician?"

"Yup."

"The Asher York with a singing voice that makes you forget your name?"

"That's the one."

"The Asher York who looks like a fucking Adonis with a guitar strapped to him?"

"Yes, Chloe. *That* Asher York," I say louder as a blush blooms on my cheeks. If she only knew just how amazing Asher York looks now with a guitar slung over his chiseled body.

He's a far cry from the guy I knew all those years ago. Hell, if the band's lead singer hadn't introduced him by name last night, I probably wouldn't have recognized him. But I would have eventually figured it out. He still has the same raspy, soulful voice, still writes lyrics filled with so much passion and heartache.

"The Asher York who would have been your brother-in-law if you hadn't smartened up and called off your engagement to Jessie?"

"Exactly." I swallow hard, a pang squeezing my heart, my stomach churning. I shouldn't feel guilty about this. I haven't spoken to Jessie in years. But I still can't help but feel like I'm betraying him by being here, even if nothing untoward has happened between Asher and me.

She blinks once. Twice. Then she steps back, glancing around at the exquisite grounds, her voice chipper. "Well, it looks like Asher's not a struggling musician anymore, is he?"

"Oh, this isn't *his* place," I correct quickly. "He's just kind of...staying here."

"Like, house sitting?"

"Not exactly. He, uh…"

A motion catches my attention. I whip my eyes to the front door, Asher appearing. A wicked smile curls his lips as he crosses his arms over his chest, leaning against the doorjamb. It takes all my willpower not to ogle his biceps. Hell, it seems to take all Chloe's willpower, too. I can't blame her. He is really nice to look at.

"When I told you it was okay for you both to crash here, I meant *inside* the house. Not on the front stoop."

"Hey, Ash." My cheeks warm as my lips kick up in the corners, the response as innate as breathing. I avert my eyes, doing everything I can to hold on to the little composure I have left so as not to make it obvious there's something more going on between us. I keep reminding myself there isn't. We've never even kissed. Not like that. So why do I feel like a hormonally crazed teenager who's run into the object of her affection during a middle school dance? "Thanks for this."

"It's nothing, Iz. You know that." He uncrosses his arms, taking a step toward me. "I was thrilled to hear your voice, considering I thought you'd be 35,000 feet in the air by now."

I lift my eyes to his. "I guess the universe had different plans."

"I guess so." A beat passes as we stay in our bubble where it's just us. Then he remembers we're not alone and clears his throat, looking to my left. "Chloe. Good to see you again. I like the hair. It suits you."

"Thanks for letting us stay here."

"Anytime. I'd never turn away a friend in need." I notice the faintest hint of a wink as he gestures for us to come in.

"Hear that?" She leans into me as we pass him, entering the foyer. "He'll never turn away a *friend* in need, Iz."

"Oh, hush. It's not like that."

"You want it to be like that, though, right?"

"Maybe," I mumble in a barely audible voice, hoping she can't hear. But the devious expression on her face tells me she did.

"I'll show you around down here, then take you up to where you'll be staying," Asher announces.

"Great!" I respond brightly, spinning around to face him.

"Great…," he repeats, his voice full of uncertainty as he eyes me, my overly enthusiastic reaction presumably catching him off-guard. That's the downside of trying to hide things from someone you once knew so well. They'll know in a heartbeat when you're acting out of character. Just like I am now.

"So, the tour?" Chloe asks, stepping forward.

"Right. This way." He turns around, and I can't help but stare at his backside. It doesn't matter that he's wearing a white linen shirt and a pair of loose-fitting shorts. I can still make out the definition of his muscles through his clothes. I thought the dimples on his face were addictive. They have nothing on those right above his waistline.

"Come on, Izzy." Chloe grabs my arm, snapping me out of my mental undressing. I stumble, my face burning, but I push down any embarrassment from getting caught ogling him. We follow him into the spacious open living area that contains the kitchen, an informal dining space, as well as a sitting area, complete with large-screen TV and what I can only imagine is a state-of-the-art sound system.

The entire place boasts high ceilings, neutral walls and furniture, the space bathed in natural light. Based on the décor, I never would have guessed *who* owned this house. It's muted and understated. Apart from a glass display case in the corner of the living room containing a handful of Grammys that Chloe pays no attention to, nothing indicates this is home to Fallen Grace's recording studio.

Asher leads us down a long corridor, showing Chloe the game room, library, workout room, and the wine "cellar", even though I struggle to call it a cellar since it's on the ground floor. I feign interest in the tour, not wanting to make it too obvious I've been here before, although it's only a matter of time until I'm forced to come clean.

As we leave the theater room, I expect him to show her the one remaining space — the recording studio. Instead, he heads back toward the foyer. Grabbing our bags, he leads us up the stairs and down what he referred to as the guest wing.

After showing Chloe to her room, he turns to me, pulling my roll-aboard a little farther down the hallway, opening the door into a luxurious space that would rival even a five-star hotel. Lush, four-poster bed. Fireplace.

Magnificent view. Ensuite bathroom I imagine contains a jetted tub.

"I hope these accommodations are up to your satisfaction." He enters behind me, setting my suitcase on an ottoman sitting below one of the windows overlooking the patio, the Las Vegas skyline on the horizon, majestic mountains stretching beyond it.

"I suppose it'll do," I joke, shifting on my feet. "At least it's only for one night."

"You're a resourceful girl. I'm sure you'll survive these inferior quarters." His eyes shine as they trace over my face with amusement, his smile wide. Then he steps back. "I'll let you get settled. I'm about to fire up the grill and make some burgers."

"Burgers? Are they—"

"Dad's recipe? You'd better believe it."

I place a hand on my hip, and his gaze floats to the sliver of exposed skin between my jeans and my shirt. "So he finally decided you were trustworthy enough to be given it?"

"Sure did," he replies boastfully, jutting out his chest. "Of course, it took quitting my decent-paying, respectable job, with great benefits and summers off, and moving out to California for him to share it. Said if things got bad, I could at least sell the recipe to make a bit of money." He winks, the gesture causing my knees to weaken.

"I'm glad you didn't have to resort to that. Your father's recipe should stay in the family." I pat my stomach. "Although I hope you have enough. It's been years since I've had one of your father's world-famous burgers. I may eat my weight in them."

"If I have to run to the store to get more ingredients, I'll do it. Can't have you leaving...unsatisfied."

My mouth grows dry at the innuendo, every cell in my body humming with the need to know all the ways Asher can satisfy me. I imagine he'd be able to do so in a manner no man before him has. In a manner no man after him will again. But that's all this can be. A fantasy. Nothing more.

With a smirk, he turns, his footsteps sounding his retreat. I go to my suitcase, about to unpack, when his deep voice fills the space. "Hey, Izzy?"

I whirl around, meeting his dark eyes swimming with deep indecision, the pendulum still swinging madly within. He licks his lips, squinting, searching for an answer that remains out of reach.

Then he exhales, his expression softening. "I'm glad you're here. *Really* glad."

He doesn't wait for me to reply, spinning around and disappearing down the hallway.

"I'm in so much trouble," I murmur to myself.

Chapter Eight

"WHEN WERE YOU going to tell me you've been getting all chummy with Asher York?" Chloe bites out the second I pull back the door to my room after changing into the only bathing suit I brought with me — a revealing black bikini that seems to make my already ample chest seem even more voluptuous. As if I'm doing it intentionally for Asher.

Maybe I am.

"Have you been waiting outside my room this entire time?"

"No." She grabs my arm, ushering me back into my room and closing the door. "But I figured twenty minutes would give you enough time to shave all your naughty bits to clear a landing strip." Dropping her grip on me, she sweeps her gaze over me, a smirk pulling on her mouth. "I was right."

I wrap my arms over my stomach, trying to hide my body, but my sheer, white coverup doesn't help much in that area. "Don't get your hopes up. There will be no landing."

"Why? I saw the way you looked at him."

"Chloe," I begin, but she doesn't let me say another word.

"And I saw the way he looked at you. How long has this been going on?"

Sighing, I collapse onto the bed. "Less than twenty-four hours." Although one could argue it's been going on since my freshman year of college.

"How?" She sits next to me, frowning, her brow wrinkled. "We've spent our entire weekend together. I'm pretty sure I would have noticed you talking to Asher. Hell, pretty sure Bernadette would have noticed, too. She would have included it in the gossip section of one of her daily 'Bachelorette News' emails she's been sending."

"Please tell me you don't actually read those."

She shrugs. "I may have fed her a fake story or two. But that's irrelevant. What's the deal with you and Asher?"

"No deal. We ran into each other last night," I explain, looking ahead with an unfocused gaze.

"Last night? When?"

"My body still thinks it's working the night shift, so I ended up going out and found an Irish pub with a live band. It was a nice change after the thumping club music we've been forced to endure this weekend."

"You mean you haven't been enjoying all that electronic crap?" she mocks in faux disbelief.

Brushing off her comment, I continue. "I went inside to have a beer and unwind. Imagine my surprise when the lead singer of the band performing announced a special guest by the name of Asher York. After he finished singing, he noticed me in the crowd and came up to me. We ended up hanging out."

"But you've been here before," she remarks, as I suspected she would.

Chloe has one of those analytical minds that doesn't miss much. It's what makes her one hell of a gossip columnist. She can smell a story before it even starts. I've lost count of the number of celebrity pregnancies she's accurately predicted before they've been announced to the public. Hell, there were a few she knew about before the celebrity's own publicist was made aware.

"After last call, we went to get a bite to eat." My lips tick up into a smile. "Then he wasn't ready for our night together to end, so he brought me back here."

"And what did you two do when you got here?" She waggles her brows.

"Played the piano," I answer.

"I bet you did."

"We did. Then we watched the sunrise before he drove me back to the hotel."

"So you mean to tell me you spent all night with Asher York… And not the Asher York you knew those years ago, but *that* Asher York." She points toward the closed door. "You're trying to tell me you spent all night with him, played piano, watched the sunrise, and nothing happened?"

"Precisely."

She pinches her lips together. "Did you *want* something to happen?"

"I don't know, Chloe." I get up from the bed, pacing as I attempt to make sense of my warring emotions. "The entire time I dated Jessie, I never once thought of Asher this way. Never looked at him this way." Until the day I realized the truth.

"I find that hard to believe," she mutters.

"Why?"

She rolls her eyes. "I may not have gone to college with you, but I saw how you guys were. Even back then. And I wasn't the only one. Hell, at your own engagement party, you spent most of the night hanging out with Asher."

77

"Because Jessie got drunk at the Sox game earlier in the day. Asher was only trying to make up for his brother's lack of self-control."

"Still…" Standing, she shrugs before crossing her arms in front of her. "You guys have always been good together."

"We've always been friends."

She approaches. "What changed?"

I point toward the door, just as she did a few seconds ago. "Have you *seen* him? You just admitted you've noticed the changes."

"He's definitely got an incredible body now." She giggles. "And that hair… He's got that sexy Johnny Depp hair. And you know how much I love me some Johnny Depp. And so do you. Bet you'd love to tug on that. Am I right?" She nudges me, passing me a devious smirk that has me cracking a smile in less than a second.

"Maybe."

Her playfulness fades as she peers at me with all the sincerity I've come to expect from my lifelong friend. "So what's stopping you?"

"Oh, I don't know." I throw my hands up, my voice laden with sarcasm. "Maybe the fact I was once engaged to his brother. And not a brother he doesn't get along with. A brother who's also his best friend. He'd never betray Jessie like that. And even if he would…"

"You hate the idea of doing anything that would jeopardize their relationship," she finishes.

She knows me better than most people. She was the first person I went to when I found out I was adopted. She made me see it didn't change anything. That I still had a loving family, even if we didn't share DNA. Learning you're adopted makes you see family in a different light. Makes you treasure it more. My stomach roils at the idea of being the cause of any strife between Asher and Jessie. Which is why I cut ties with them all those years ago. My heart had splintered in two different directions. It was better to walk away before it was beyond repair.

"Do you blame me?"

On a long exhale, Chloe drapes an arm over my shoulders, pulling me back onto the bed. "I certainly don't. But you also don't need to sit here, making long-term plans for a future. Hell, you don't even have to make plans for tomorrow, since we're headed back home... God willing. Have fun and enjoy your time with Asher." The seriousness and compassion in her expression wanes, her mouth kicking up into a mischievous grin once more. "And if something should happen, you know what they say about this town, don't you?" She stands, heading toward the door. "What happens here..."

"I know. I know. Stays here," I finish, dragging myself to my feet.

"Exactly. Now, let's go enjoy one more day in the sun before we have to return to the frozen tundra of Manhattan." She loops her arm through mine, pulling me out of the room and down the stairs.

The instant we turn the corner into the open kitchen, my heart speeds up at the sight of Asher standing in front of the island. I can't stop my lips from parting, my eyes drawn to the flexing muscles in his forearms as he works the meat into patties. It's a simple act, one that shouldn't be considered erotic in any sense, but it sets my body aflame.

"All right, Asher," Chloe says, flashing me a sly grin, noticing my stare trained on him. "Whose house is this? Izzy said you're not house sitting, so what *are* you doing in a place like this?"

"Don't think I can afford it myself?" He catches my eye, winking, which only serves to turn me into a ball of putty. God, this man can wink.

"Last I heard, you were playing bars in LA, trying to make it big." This statement surprises me since *I* didn't even know he'd left Boston.

"Maybe I've made it big."

"Have you?"

It's silent for a moment while he considers Chloe's question. Then he returns his attention to the hamburger mixture, continuing to form the patties.

"Not yet, but I'm one step closer."

"What do you mean?" She looks from Asher to me, searching for some explanation. My gaze flashes to the display case in the corner of the living room containing the Grammy awards. Noticing my gesture, she turns, walking toward it. When she realizes who they belong to, her reaction mirrors what mine was. Mouth falling open. Dazed stare. Body stiffening.

"You're in Fallen Grace?" she all but shrieks, whirling around.

"Certainly not." A low chuckle rumbles through him. "They're not really my style."

With an unaffected attitude I find attractive, considering most men in his position would probably brag about their good fortune, Asher recounts the story of how he came to form a partnership with one of the most successful music acts in the world, demonstrating the same humility he always exhibited toward everything.

"It goes to show that sometimes good things happen when we least expect it," he remarks thoughtfully once he finishes telling Chloe the story he relayed to me last night. Or this morning.

Heat washes over my face, and I lift my eyes to find the source. Has he always looked at me this way? Have his nostrils always flared as his gaze rakes over my body? Have his pupils always dilated with hunger as he steals a glimpse of my cleavage? Has this electricity always existed?

Maybe he acts this way around all women. Maybe he's behaving like this because he's been stuck in a house with a boy band for God knows how long and I'm the first relatively attractive female he's seen in ages. The reasons for his unabashed admiration of my body don't matter. All that does is that I've been given the gift of spending another day with him. Maybe Chloe's right. Maybe I need to stop worrying about the potential ramifications and just let the cards fall where they may.

"So…" Asher clears his throat, looking away. "What can I get you to drink?"

I exhale. A drink is exactly what I need to help settle these nervous butterflies flitting in my stomach.

Once we all have a beer in hand, he grabs the plate of burgers and leads us toward the open French doors. As I follow behind him, I can't help but admire his long, toned legs, the way his plaid swim trunks fall from his hips, the faint outline of more tattoos underneath his white, linen shirt.

"Lincoln!" he calls out once we emerge onto the pergola-covered patio, forcing me out of my thoughts. "Get off your phone and be social." He lowers his voice, addressing us. "He'll be done soon, I hope."

He sets the plate on a table beside the grill. I inhale the charcoal aroma, the combination of the smell and being here with Asher reminiscent of the summers at Grams' lake house. Now if only she were here, regaling us with yet another one of her outrageous stories, my heart would be full. Then again, it's best she's not. She'd probably force us all to do paddleboard yoga in the pool. Or she'd go skinny-dipping. Grams was never shy about the naked form, which served to embarrass Jessie and make Asher laugh.

"Who's *he*?" Chloe asks. Her eyes flame, presumably over the idea of one of the band members being here.

"Lincoln Moore," he explains as he places the burgers onto the grill, which causes my stomach to growl. My mouth salivates in anticipation of what I know will be one hell of a burger. "We went to college together. In fact, he was a workaholic back then, too. Constantly studying. He was one of those guys who lived according to the motto 'work hard, play hard'."

"I like to think that now it's 'work hard, play even harder'," a deep voice says, and I look in its direction, sucking in a sharp inhale of air when I see the figure approaching Chloe from behind.

I may have been a few yards away, but I'd be able to pick out the man who had my best friend in a passionate embrace in the hotel from a lineup. The mysterious, deep-set eyes with swirls of caramel and gold. The full lips that quirk up in amusement. And the tall, muscular physique that easily has a foot over Chloe. She was right. They appear to be as opposite as you can get. But does that matter?

Unable to move, Chloe stares at me with wide eyes, as if waiting for me to confirm that her suspicions are correct, that the enthralling voice belongs to the man she thinks it does.

This day just got *much* more interesting.

"Chloe, Izzy…," Asher begins, oblivious to the growing tension sizzling in the air. "This is my friend, Lincoln. Lincoln, this is Izzy and—"

"Dick Girl," Lincoln finishes, stepping in front of Chloe, his gaze glued to her.

"Dick Girl?" Asher furrows his brow, his stare ping-ponging between them. If Chloe hadn't told me about his nickname for her, I'd be just as confused. "Do you two know each other?"

"We've had the...pleasure."

I notice a shiver roll through Chloe's body, a strange response for someone who normally has no reaction to the opposite sex.

"Or perhaps I should say *I've* had the pleasure of experiencing her sharp tongue."

Damn. Now I can see what has Chloe acting so out of character. This guy is as smooth as a twenty-year-old scotch. And seemingly just as mature, which is what she needs.

"Yes." She holds her head high, thrusting her hand out toward him in a manner you'd expect to find in a business meeting, not a chance encounter between two people with off-the-charts chemistry. "It's nice to see you again, to *formally* meet you, Lincoln."

He takes her hand in his. Instead of shaking it, he brings it to his lips, not peeling his eyes off hers as he places a soft kiss on the skin. "Likewise, Chloe. I didn't think we'd see each other again."

"Either did I."

"Funny how that keeps happening, isn't it? How we keep...bumping into each other. If I didn't know any better, I'd think someone, some*thing* wants us to keep seeing each other."

I feel the heat of Asher's breath on my neck, followed by that low, husky voice. "I could say the same about you."

I turn to face him, the hair on my nape standing on end when I see the unyielding desire in his eyes. I bring my beer to my lips, taking a long sip. "Is that so?"

He slowly nods. "That's so." His expression changes, this one more curious than needy. He closes the distance between us. "Why do you think that is?"

"I don't know," I answer honestly, my chest rising and falling in a quicker rhythm.

"Me, either. But a part of me wants to find out."

"And the other part?" I barely manage to squeak out.

"Is so fucking torn." He rakes his hand through his hair, retreating into himself. Just as he did on more than one occasion last night.

"Me, too."

Chapter Nine

"SO, WHAT'S NEXT on the agenda for game night?" I ask in a bright voice after we cleaned up all the Jenga blocks that clattered to the ground, thanks to Lincoln getting cocky and not paying attention as he placed one, slightly skewed, on top of the tower.

The afternoon sped by in a fog of burgers, bachelorette party stories, and a fun game of Jenga, something I haven't played since my Introduction to Nursing Science class when my professor had us work together in groups to prevent the tower from toppling over, equating it to the teamwork necessary in the nursing profession.

"Game night?" Chloe scrunches her nose, her lip curled up.

"Yeah. Game night."

"Oh no." She quickly shakes her head, her reaction akin to one you might expect if accused of a horrific crime. "This isn't game night. That's something bored, married couples do to mask the fact that they have nothing in common with each other. The arrogant husband acts as if he's a know-it-all anytime his wife answers a question wrong in Trivial Pursuit. And during a rousing game of Taboo, she realizes exactly how little her husband listens to her. No thanks. Not interested."

I pass her a wry smile. "Not all games are boring."

Able to sense the wheels spinning, she narrows her eyes on me. "What did you have in mind?"

"You'll see." I jump up and walk into the house without a single look back.

Once inside, I head straight for the game room. I'm not sure how everyone will react to my idea, but we're all adults. If I hadn't consumed the number of beers I have, I probably wouldn't suggest this, but I need *something* to cut through the constant push and pull between Asher and me. An icebreaker of sorts. In my experience, this game has always been great at doing just that.

"I told you, Chloe," I say once I return to the patio, placing a box on the wicker coffee table. "Game night doesn't always have to be boring. What do you guys think? Want to take things up a notch?" I float my eyes around our little party sitting on a pair of couches placed on either side of the coffee table, girls on one side and guys on the other. When my gaze stops on Asher, he swallows hard, pulling his bottom lip between his teeth. "Or are you too chicken?"

"Never Have I Ever?" Chloe turns her nose up as she reads the words printed on the box.

"Why not? I thought you were an open book, that you had no shame."

"I don't."

"Then what's stopping you?" I steal a glimpse at Lincoln before looking back at her.

As day turned into night, their flirting has become a bit more obvious. The angst is killing me. I can only imagine how it's affecting Chloe.

"Fine." She pushes out a sigh, feigning annoyance, but I can tell she likes the idea. "But if we're going to play this, I'll need a fresh beer." She starts to stand, but Lincoln stops her with a gentle hand on her arm.

"I got it." His gaze lingers on her a beat longer than normal before shifting his attention to the rest of us. "I'll grab another round for everyone. I have a feeling we all may need it."

I watch as he disappears into the house. I probably should have told him I didn't want another beer, considering I'm already tipsy, but it's my last night in Vegas. Might as well have some fun while I still can.

"I'm going to take advantage of this break and go change." Chloe stands, her eyes averted as she walks away.

"Are you sure you're not planning to take advantage of something else?" I call after her, even though putting on something warmer sounds appealing now that the temperature has dipped significantly from earlier. Asher warned me it would happen. The second the sun disappeared beyond the horizon, it was like someone turned off a heating lamp, an instant chill setting in.

She waves me off, not even acknowledging me as she steps inside, closing the French doors behind her. I slowly shift my eyes back to Asher's, not sure what I'll see, whether it will be warmth and endearment or purposeful distance. When I peer into them, I see something else. Something I can't quite explain. He gazes upon me with affection, but it's so much more pronounced. More charged. More intense.

Standing from his position across the coffee table from me, he heads toward me, each step causing my pulse to kick up a little. He assumes the open spot beside me, draping his arm along the back of the couch. He leans toward me, his scent wafting into my nostrils, a natural aphrodisiac that has me wanting to burrow my nose into the crook of his neck.

"What do you know about those two?" he asks in a low voice.

87

"Not much." I fidget with my hands, the huskiness in his tone and lust in his eyes unnerving me. I hate not being able to read this man, one whom I once thought I knew as well as my own boyfriend at the time. Maybe even better. "Chloe mentioned she kept running into some guy all weekend. At the club. Then the restaurant bar. Then in the elevator this morning. Up until you introduced him to her, she didn't even know his name."

He lifts a single brow. "She didn't?"

"No. She didn't. Even though when I walked into the lobby to meet her, she was a breath away from kissing him."

He pulls back, tilting his head. "They've kissed?"

"*Almost.* But some drunk college kids bumped into her before they could seal the deal, so to speak."

"She was willing to kiss him without knowing his name?"

"Does a name really matter if you have a connection?" I push my hair behind my ear.

I should stop, knowing my words may very well spark Asher's guilt and pull him back. My guilt is pulling me back, too. But if I don't say it now, I'll always wonder *what if.* I've suffered through years of *what if.* No more.

"Does anything really matter if you feel a connection? Especially when finding someone you click with seems to be such a rarity these days. Maybe that's why so many relationships fail. They let all the outside noise cloud what they know can be an amazing thing. They let all the reasons they shouldn't be together overpower the one reason they should."

"And what would that be?"

"That they *feel* something."

He peers deep into my eyes. I physically feel the indecision, the contradicting desires tugging him in two different directions. One keeping him firmly in place, reminding him who I am. The other pushing him forward, imploring him to take a leap of faith. No matter what he chooses, he risks losing something. It's just a matter of what's more important.

When he tears his gaze from mine, his head hanging as he shakes it, I know the answer. In a sense, I've always known.

I'm about to excuse myself to find my own beer to drown myself in when his soft voice stops me.

"You're right."

I raise my eyes to his, my pulse gradually increasing as he reaches for my face. The seconds stretch to an eternity in anticipation of the touch of his hand against my skin. When I feel the subtle brush of his fingers, I sigh. It's such an innocent contact, but I love the roughness of his flesh on mine. The callouses on his fingertips from hours of playing guitar make me feel alive. More alive than I've ever been.

"I guess nothing else *should* matter." He pushes a tendril of hair behind my ear.

I lick my lips, eyes focused on his deep orbs. His gaze shifts to my mouth, pupils darkening. I notice the tightening of his muscles, his chest heaving a little more, jaw clenching and unclenching.

"But that's not the case, is it?" I squeak out as he closes the distance between us.

"One second, I tell myself it doesn't matter. That nothing else matters." He runs the pad of his thumb over my bottom lip. His caress is so soft, barely noticeable, but the way every inch of me ignites, you'd think he were touching the most intimate parts of my body, my mind, my soul.

"And the next?"

"The next, I'm reminded of what's at stake."

89

I expect him to pull away, but he doesn't. So I keep going. "And what *is* at stake?"

"Everything," he admits, his voice becoming harsher, almost like a growl. "But you know what they say, don't you?"

I shake my head. "I don't."

"The worse the odds, the bigger the reward."

"And what do you hope to be your reward?" Hypnotized, I inch closer, his breath dancing on my lips. Like Asher, I may regret this tomorrow. Hell, I may regret it in just a few minutes, but I need to stop worrying about the future. I need to just live in the moment. After all, I'm in Vegas, a city where everyone lives in the moment.

"Everything I never knew I always wanted." He pauses, then adds, "Actually, that's a lie."

He flashes his breathtaking smile. I push down the thought that it's so similar to Jessie's, apart from the dimples. Perfect white teeth framed with full, luscious lips.

His grip on my face tightening, he digs his fingers into my scalp, the raw need in the way he holds me making my hunger for him grow. "Deep down, a part of me always wanted this, but I just needed a reminder of what I'd lose if I let the chance slip away again."

"And what was that reminder?"

"Feeling you in my arms last night, Isabella." He runs a lithe finger down the curve of my face. I close my eyes, savoring the delicious tremor his touch causes. "Nothing ever felt so…perfect." He pinches my chin, bringing my lips closer to his. So close. So warm. So wanted. "*You* are perfect."

I hold my breath, bracing for him to consume every part of me.

One minute, he's on the cusp of kissing me. The next, there's a vacancy where he once was, his touch gone.

"Shit," he curses.

I fling my eyes open, disoriented. Everything seems darker than it was mere seconds ago. Asher jumps up from the couch, stalking away from me, and my heart sinks. I'm ready to berate him for all these fucked-up games he's been playing. Before I can, his distressed voice interrupts me.

"We must have blown a fuse."

My mouth snaps shut as I scan the back yard. Now I know why everything seems darker. It wasn't Asher's confusing mood that cast a shadow over us. It's because the power's off.

I stand to join him as he stares down at the pool, the lights illuminating the depths gone. As are all the lights on the patio, the entire back yard dark. Looking to the house, we realize it's also devoid of any light.

"How?"

"I don't know." He shakes his head. "I'll go check." He squeezes my arm, then places a soft kiss on my temple. It's a crappy consolation prize, considering I was hoping for more, but it'll have to do…for now.

"I'll come with you to make sure Chloe's okay." I catch up to his long strides with ease.

"Oh, I'm sure she's *more* than okay." He waggles his brows as he holds the door for me, allowing me to step into the darkened house first, the entire place eerily still.

Asher rests a protective hand on my lower back, ushering me toward the kitchen island. It's probably a good thing, considering the layout of the house is as foreign as the Palace of Versailles.

"Lincoln seems to have disappeared, too." He rummages through a drawer by the sink, finding a flashlight. "Think he's helping Chloe slip into

91

something more…comfortable?" He flicks on the flashlight, which illuminates the devious grin on his face.

"It *is* Vegas after all." I spin from him, heading in the direction of the staircase I can barely make out in the stream of light. As I approach the bottom step, I glance over my shoulder. "If you can't sin a little here, where can you?"

He catches up to me as I ascend the staircase with timid steps. "Is that what you want?" His husky voice causes the hairs on my nape to stand on end, a rush of desire pooling in my core. "To sin a little?" He narrows his gaze on mine as we crest the top of the stairs.

Emboldened, I come to a stop, angling into him. I don't move for several long seconds, sensing his composure crack, that vein in his neck throbbing with suppressed want. "Play your cards right and maybe you'll find out." I allow my words to float around him for a beat before I continue down the hallway, Asher following. I can almost taste the lust in the air between us. Tonight is about to get a lot more interesting, especially if the lights don't come back on.

Approaching Chloe's room, I notice the door is ajar. I round the corner, figuring she would have closed it if she were getting it on with Lincoln.

"There you are!" I say, heading toward where she stands by the window, still in her bathing suit. Apparently, she *has* been too preoccupied to change. When Lincoln walks out of the ensuite bathroom, I stop in my tracks. "Both of you."

"Did we blow a fuse?" Chloe asks, averting her eyes, fidgeting with her hair. Which is the Chloe tell that she's been doing something, or some*one*, she'd rather I didn't find out about.

92

"I don't know." I cross my arms over my chest. "Did you?"

"I don't think it was a fuse," Lincoln interrupts, joining Chloe by the window.

Everyone looks in his direction, following his line of sight. After watching the sunrise with Asher last night, I'm more than aware of what the view out that window should be. Instead of seeing the bright lights of the Vegas Strip, there's nothing, the only lights that of cars meandering along the streets. Everything else is barren. Deserted. Empty.

"Like I said," Lincoln continues as we all congregate around him, staring at a scene that's reminiscent of a post-apocalyptic horror film, minus the zombies feeding on human brains. "I don't think it was a fuse."

Chapter Ten

"OKAY, SO WHAT are the rules here?" Chloe asks after we've all settled back outside.

With no power, it was the most logical place to congregate, considering we have the fire pit to offer us heat and light. It's another reminder of my few summers at Grams' lake house. While there was electricity, that's where the amenities ended. No cable. No internet. No cell service. Our only form of communication with the outside world was a landline Grams put in for emergencies. I'd often hated returning to civilization, wanting to go back to how simple things were at the lake. Jessie seemed to career down the narrow roads at breakneck speed to get back to the point where our cell service would kick in.

"I've never played the board game version of this." Her expression instantly brightens. "There's one. Never have I ever played the board game version of Never Have I Ever! Do I get a point or something? Or maybe I just win game night outright and we can stop this torture?"

I roll my eyes. "You're having fun and you know it."

She bites her lower lip, looking from me to Lincoln. "Maybe."

"That's what I thought." I catch Asher's eyes as he sits beside me. There's a hint of amusement and curiosity in them while he observes me in silence. An artist studying his subject, unearthing every crevice, every valley, every subtle imperfection in order to paint her with painstaking detail. I wonder if that's what he's doing. If he's writing a song in his head. He has that look about him. Excitement. Concentration. Inspiration. I like the idea of being Asher's inspiration. His muse. The Marianne Faithful to his Mick Jagger. A much younger and more attractive Mick Jagger.

"So... The rules?" Chloe's voice cuts through.

I snap my attention back to her, ignoring the smirk drawn on her face. "It's pretty straightforward. You roll this die." I pick it up, showing it to everyone. "On each side is a symbol that corresponds to a category on the cards." I grab one from the stack to demonstrate. "Whatever you roll is what you have to say. So if I roll this male and female symbol, which is the sex and dating category, I have to say 'Never have I ever ditched a date after the first ten minutes.' If I haven't, I move my game piece forward. If I have, I take a drink. The first person to cross the finish line wins."

"Have you played this before?" she inquires.

"I didn't even know they'd made a board game out of it until I saw it in the game room."

"Then how did you know how to play?"

I grab the rule sheet out of the box and wave it in front of her. "I read the directions. Not exactly rocket science." I pass her a sardonic smile, then return my attention to our assembled group. "Okay. Who's first?"

"Since this was your lame idea, you should go first," Chloe suggests with playful arrogance.

Passing her a smug grin, I say, "Never have I ever ditched my date after the first ten minutes." I grab my beer and take a sip, indicating I have, in fact, done just that.

"You need to roll and pick a new card," Chloe insists.

"After you tell me all about the poor schmuck you ditched," Asher chimes in.

"Why? So you can tell me I should have given him a bit longer?"

"No." His gaze remains locked on me as he slowly shakes his head. "So I know what *not* to do." He clears his throat as he nervously glances around our little circle. "You know. Research. For a song maybe."

"Really?"

"Why not?" His lips quirk up into a mischievous grin. I don't think I'll ever tire of the sparkle in his dark eyes as they look upon me with wanton affection.

"Stop cheating and roll," Chloe admonishes.

"Fine." I grab the die and toss it onto the table. It lands on a symbol of the earth, which means the subject could be anything. Taking a card off the top of the pile, I read the corresponding phrase. "Never have I ever gone streaking." Rolling my eyes, I grab a red game piece and move it forward a square. "Well, that's an easy one because it's never happened. Who's next?"

"I'll go," Asher pipes up, reaching for the die.

Chloe whistles when it lands on the symbol for sex and dating. "I have a feeling this is going to get interesting fast."

"You and me both," I mutter.

Asher chuckles when he reads the phrase off the card. "Never have I ever kissed a celebrity. Yeah. Definitely haven't done that." He takes his green game piece and pushes it forward a spot.

"You mean you haven't gotten in on some of the orgies Fallen Grace is rumored to host?" Chloe jokes.

He looks up at her, brows scrunched. "Is that really a rumor?"

"Fallen Grace fans aren't our target audience, but I keep a finger on all celebrity gossip. Rumor is two of the guys are gay and in a relationship with each other."

"Do I want to ask which two?" He leans back, brushing his thumb against his bottom lip, which makes me salivate, remembering how he'd caressed my lip like that.

Chloe squints, trying to pull some names out of her memory. I have no idea how she keeps all these celebrities straight. How she remembers who's dating whom, who's in whatever band, who's starring in whatever movie. Then again, she says the same thing about my line of work, amazed at how much I do as a nurse.

"I think Mason and Ellis."

Asher chokes on his beer, coughing a few times. "Mason and Ellis?" he grinds out, clearing his throat. "Did you seriously say Mason and Ellis are rumored to be gay and into each other?"

"Again, this isn't my area of expertise, so—"

Asher chuckles. "They are not gay." His laughter grows, his face reddening, tears dotting the corners of his eyes. I can't remember the last time I've heard him laugh like this. "Actually, none of the guys are, but Mason and Ellis? They're so far from being gay, they're not even in the same hemisphere." He draws in a deep breath to get his laughter under control. "Not that being gay's a bad thing. In my opinion, love is love, no matter who it's between. Well, within reason. Those child brides being forced to marry some sixty-year-old dude is disconcerting, but that's beside the point. Trust me. With the number of women Mason and Ellis bring back here, you'd think they were considering starting their own brothel."

"So no wedding bells between them in the future?" Chloe presses.

"Certainly not. Now, who's next?" He looks around the circle.

"I think Chloe should go," I offer.

"This ought to be good," Lincoln interjects, having remained silent during the rest of our exchange.

His aloof attitude reminds me of Asher. They both have a mysteriousness about them. An analytical way they observe the world around them, carefully selecting their words before saying anything.

It's a stark contrast to most men I've had the unfortunate displeasure of dating. Men who felt the need to impress me with so much bravado, constantly talking themselves up, not once asking me a single question. I didn't think it bothered me. I don't like talking about myself, especially considering the normal questions most people ask on a date — What do you like to do? What's your family like? How many brothers and sisters? The instant I tell someone I'm adopted, things change. There's a look of sympathy on their faces. I hate that.

The next few hours pass in a mixture of laughter, increasing sexual tension, and consumption of more beers than we should, but what choice do we have? The power is out, so those beers will only go bad. We're simply doing our civic duty of saving the beers from meeting an unfortunate demise.

At first, I was unsure how everyone would react to this game. To my surprise, it's gone over well, so much so that even when Lincoln is the first to cross the finish line, we continue, throwing the die and going around the circle, drinking if we've done whatever is on the card. We've even reverted to some of the original rules from when we played in college, requiring others to drink if they've done whatever was said, even if it's not their turn.

Once our laughter dies down after Lincoln told everyone how his ex cockblocked him by using her cat to curse him, I look at the coffee table, frowning. "We're out of cards."

I hate the idea of our game ending. While there's still some tension between Asher and me, the constant push and pull has evaporated. Like he's decided to just let go, allow the night to take us where it's meant to. We've returned to the way things have always been. Easy conversation. Laughing at ridiculous stories. Not wanting the night to end. Of course, the things we've talked about have been much more personal, but that's the nature of the game. And something I was hoping for anyway.

"Maybe it's time we go off-script," Chloe suggests. I whip my eyes toward her, a single brow cocked. "We stopped with the board game part of this a while back." She gestures at the discarded board. "Maybe it's time to make things more interesting and ask different kinds of questions."

"What kinds of questions did you have in mind?" I ask.

"I don't know. Something deeper. A little more…personal."

"*Therapist* personal or *sexy* personal?"

"Therapist personal." She holds her head high, then shifts her eyes to Lincoln before adding, "And sexy personal."

In a heartbeat, a charge is sparked. It's no longer an easygoing, albeit slightly risqué game among friends, both old and new. We don't have to share our thoughts with one another to know we're all thinking the same thing — this has the possibility to change everything.

"I'm okay with that," Asher states. "We're all adults. Not much makes me uncomfortable." His demeanor is calm, maybe even a little intrigued. He's not pulling away like I thought he would.

"We *are* all adults, aren't we?" I muse.

"What's going through that brain of yours?" Chloe asks, able to sense the wheels spinning in my head.

I look into the distance where the skyline of Las Vegas should be illuminated, but it's not, the entire world shrouding us in relative darkness, as if we're in a bubble where the events of tonight won't matter when the lights come back on. Where we can give in to our deepest desires with no consequences.

I grab a flashlight off the table and proceed into the house without saying a single word. Chloe wants to take our game to the next level. Well, we still need a pair of dice.

Making my way to my room, I open the bachelorette goody bag Bernadette put together, which contained mostly inappropriate items, including a vibrator. Apparently marrying the guy who knocked you up in college doesn't always equal sexual satisfaction, as was evident by her constant flirting with anything with a pulse. I toss butt plugs, eye masks, and body paint into my suitcase, finally finding what I'm looking for. Wrapping my fingers around them, I hurry down the stairs and return to the patio, three sets of expectant eyes meeting mine.

"What's going on?" Chloe asks.

"Like Asher said…" I hold my head high, despite the small ball of doubt forming in my stomach at the possibility no one will want to go along with this. But if we can't throw caution to the wind, can't take a risk during a blackout in Sin City, when can we? "We're all adults, correct?"

"Yes...," everyone answers, their voices laced with curiosity.

"I'm declaring a circle of trust...a bubble, so to speak." I wave my arms in a circle, drawing an invisible dome around us. "I submit for your consideration a new take on Never Have I Ever."

"I'm not sure I want to know what this new take is." Asher's voice is playful as he crosses his arms in front of his broad chest.

"You probably don't, considering it's how I met your brother..." The second I see his face blanch, I regret saying that. We hadn't brought up Jessie all evening. It's been as if there never was a Jessie. Regardless, I continue, recovering quickly. "But circle of trust." I waver on my legs, thanks to all the beers I consumed throughout the afternoon and evening.

When I'm met with more blank stares, I explain the rules. "We'll go around in a circle, saying something we've never done. If someone says they've never done something and you have, you drink. The changed rules apply to the person speaking. For example, if I say 'Never have I ever shot Abraham Lincoln', obviously no one here will drink. In that case, we go to the penalty round."

I extend my hand, revealing a pair of dice. But they're not your traditional dice. Considering our goody bags were filled with nothing but sex toys, these dice are sexy, too, one die containing an action, the other a body part.

Chloe looks at the dice in my hands. "How do we know whose thigh we have to bite?"

I swipe my nearly empty beer off the table, finishing it. "That's what this is for. Whoever the bottle lands on is the lucky, or perhaps *unlucky*, winner..."

101

"I am *not* biting Asher's thigh," Lincoln bellows, his voice deep.

"And I am not..." Asher grabs the dice and rolls them, "sucking his finger."

With an over-exaggerated sigh, I fall back onto the couch beside Asher. "Men. This game is much more fun with only girls. They don't care about this shit. We have no problem licking each other's tongues."

Asher and Lincoln simultaneously dart their wide eyes to mine, their bodies growing rigid at the mention of two women kissing. Just as I suspected would happen. Boys will always be boys.

"But fine," I continue, doing my best not to pay attention to Asher as he adjusts his shorts. "How about this? Everyone gets one free pass. Of course, just say something you know at least one other person sitting here has already done and you won't have to worry about spinning the bottle. Unless you *want* to..." I retrieve the dice and roll them, "blow on someone's neck." Lifting my bottle, I glance around our circle expectantly. "Are you all in?"

"Blackout Club," Chloe mutters.

"What?" I tilt my head.

"The first rule of Blackout Club..."

"You don't talk about Blackout Club," the guys finish in unison, and the lightbulb goes off over my head. Every guy knows a *Fight Club* reference when they hear one. They'd probably get their man card revoked if they didn't.

"Exactly." Chloe floats her eyes back to mine, raising her own beer. "Like you said, this is a bubble. We're all consenting adults... *Single* consenting adults. I'm in."

"Me, too." When Asher lifts his bottle, I exhale a tiny breath. I wouldn't have put money on him agreeing to this. I just worry when the see-saw he's riding hits the ground, it will be with so much force and velocity everything will come crumbling down.

We shift our attention to Lincoln. He raises his beer and we all clink bottles, sealing the deal. "Let the games begin."

Chapter Eleven

"WHAT ARE YOU doing? Contemplating the meaning of life?" Lincoln quips as Asher stares into the distance, brows scrunched in deep concentration.

The evening took a curious turn once we started playing our own version of Never Have I Ever. While there's no rule we say something personal or risqué, it didn't matter. It was assumed we'd go in that direction. Add in all the alcohol we've consumed, and it's become increasingly difficult to think of things we're certain someone else has done. My only saving grace has been the fact that Chloe and I are childhood friends. We have an advantage over everyone else. Correction... *I* have an advantage over everyone else, considering I also know Asher pretty well.

"I'm thinking," he answers. "Everything I come up with has been said."

"At the rate you're going, my buzz will be gone by the time you finally say something," I joke, taking another sip of my beer. "Hell, I may even have gray hair by then."

"I thought you already did," Chloe jabs. "Pretty sure I saw one the other day when I was helping you curl your hair. You are less than a year away from turning thirty."

"Oh, hush. It was merely sun-kissed." I wink.

"That's the story you're sticking with?"

"Damn straight it is."

Our laugher echoes in the stillness of the night as we turn our attention back to Asher, who's tapping a finger against his bottom lip.

"Okay, that's it." I grab the dice and shove them at him. "New rule. If you fail to say anything in the time allotted...say, a minute...it's an automatic roll of the dice and spin of the bottle. So let 'em roll, Ash."

"That's not fair." He glances toward Lincoln. "Isn't it unconstitutional or illegal for laws to be applied retroactively?"

"Generally speaking, yes."

"See." He smirks, crossing his arms in front of his chest, an air of superiority about him. "So that rule doesn't apply to me."

"Although, due to the grievous nature of your offense, I'd be inclined to agree with Izzy in this instance," Lincoln continues.

I smile at him. "Thank you. I knew there was something I liked about you."

"You bet."

"Traitor," Asher quips.

"Can you blame me?" Lincoln shoots back. "You're messing with the flow of the game. And like Izzy pointed out..." He lifts his beer. "I'm *also* losing my buzz. There should be some sort of punishment for that."

I face Asher, grinning. "You definitely deserve to be punished."

He twists toward me, his hungry eyes skating over my chest before meeting my gaze. "Is that right?"

My voice is husky as I lean closer, my breath dancing against his mouth. "Oh, that's right."

His jaw clenches so hard I'm confident it'll lock in place. I edge closer still, his body growing more and more rigid with each painful second that passes. When I'm a whisper away from his lips, I pause. All it would take would be a flick of the tongue and I'd have my first taste. But as much as I want that, I want this more. The knowledge that I drive this man to the brink of all reason.

Abruptly pulling back, I extend my hand toward him, grinning. "Better roll the dice."

His eyes are a pool of desire and lust as they bore holes into the fiber of my being. He's never looked at me with such unabashed desperation. Such primal craving. It's the way every woman wants a man to look at her. Like he can't go another minute without crushing my body to his, our souls intertwining, never to separate again.

"Very well." Not looking anywhere else, he slowly reaches toward my outstretched hand. His fingers tease the flesh of my palm, tracing a light circle against it before scooping up the dice.

I exhale the breath I was holding, my teeth chattering as I sink back into the couch, needing it to support me. Then he abruptly erases the distance between us. My heart catches in my throat, swallowing my gasp.

"But if this bottle lands on you, I'd be hard-pressed to call that a punishment." He's shameless as he drinks me in, starting with my dark eyes, along my lips, down my neck, settling for several long beats on my chest. "More like a reward." I grow lightheaded as he nears, breath by excruciating breath. "A very…" He brings his finger up to my mouth, and I plump out my bottom lip. "Very…" His touch skims my jawline and toward my ear, pushing my hair over one shoulder.

When he dips toward me, his heat skates along my neck and I fist the cushion below me, needing something, anything, to keep me grounded when I'm certain I'm about to blast off into oblivion. I don't even care that Chloe and Lincoln are witnessing this very public, very erotic exchange. We're in a bubble. There are no rules. No tomorrow. Just right now. And right now, I want more of Asher's words.

"Welcome reward," he finishes, pausing before retreating. I shoot my wide eyes to his, my chest heaving in labored pants like I'd just run a marathon in under two hours, setting a world record. "Two can play this game, Izzy."

Acting as unaffected as always, he refocuses his attention on the game, shifting empty beer bottles off the coffee table to make room for the dice. I attempt to fight the blush warming my cheeks, but I fear, even in the relative darkness, it's obvious. Chloe catches my eye, grinning slyly. I return her raised brow with one of my own, the two of us holding an entire conversation without saying a single word.

When Asher rolls, I turn my attention to him, unusually invested in the outcome. A part of me wants the dice to land on KISS and LIPS, then the bottle to stop on me so he can finish what he started. But I have a feeling even a kiss won't be enough to extinguish the fire burning inside me. Seeing him last night sparked the embers that had been crackling for years. Not even the most skilled of firefighters could extinguish this flame.

The dice come to a stop, and we all lean forward to peer in the darkness, cheers and whistles erupting when we see BITE and EAR displayed prominently.

"I bet Asher really knows how to bite an ear." Chloe playfully nudges Lincoln.

Maintaining his air of mystery, his expression remains even as he curves toward her. He brushes her hair behind her ear and whispers something. What I wouldn't give to be a fly circling them. But the raw electricity coming off their bodies would zap it in a heartbeat.

I can't quite figure out what it is about him that has Chloe turning into putty when she's spent the past decade remaining detached from every man who showed even a modicum of interest. All I know about him is he's a lawyer, and surprisingly also lives in Manhattan. Oh, and that a cat put a cockblocking curse on him.

But the fact that she knows so little about him doesn't seem to matter to her. Maybe all that stuff is inconsequential. Maybe the past doesn't matter. Maybe all that does is the connection. The chemistry. The electricity. Like I told Asher earlier.

"Well, let's see who the winner is." Asher swipes the bottle off the table and spins. It slides and skitters before slowing, our eyes following its journey until it finally comes to a stop.

On me.

I stare at the bottle, trying to silence my libido, who's shaking her pom-poms and doing a victory lap around the field.

"Well then. I guess it's time I serve my sentence."

Heat blooms on my cheeks as I slowly face him. "I guess it is." I pick at the label on my beer bottle, failing miserably at keeping my cool now that I'm seconds away from feeling Asher's mouth on my skin in something much more intimate than a chaste kiss on my forehead.

"I'll take that." The throaty timbre of his voice causes my stomach to clench, my thighs involuntarily squeezing together. A puppet to whatever he commands, I allow him to take the bottle from me and place it on the table. "Now, where were we?"

When he curves toward me, every muscle tightens, my body turning to stone. I can't remember how to breathe, the promise of this man nibbling on my ear sending lust shooting through my veins. I try to tell myself it's due to the lack of intimacy in my life lately. Or the beers I've consumed. Or because we're stuck in a blackout in a city notorious for encouraging people to sin. But deep down, those things are completely inconsequential. I'd be this desperate for Asher regardless of the circumstances. I've *been* this desperate for Asher since the first time I heard his raspy voice come over the speakers at a club in Boston.

"Oh yes. I believe I was about to serve my sentence." His breath tickles my skin, every excruciatingly long second torturing me even more. I'm so on edge. So delirious. So hungry. "But can it really be considered a punishment when I'm getting so much pleasure out of this?"

Before I can utter a response, his teeth lightly clamp onto my earlobe. Sparks shoot through me and I arch my back. I do everything to fight back a moan, losing the battle the second he swipes his tongue along my flesh. If this is how I react to a slight nibble of my ear, I fear what his kiss would do to me.

Then again, I have a feeling I already know that answer.

His kiss will ruin me in all the ways I want to be ruined.

And in all the ways I'm scared of, too.

Chapter Twelve

MAYBE INSTITUTING A time limit wasn't as great an idea as I originally thought. With our heads becoming foggy…apart from Chloe, who's only had a couple of beers over the course of the afternoon and evening…it's been increasingly difficult to come up with something no one's said in the time allotted. Which has resulted in more throwing of the dice and spinning of the bottle.

"Never have I ever gotten so drunk I had to be carried out of a bar," Asher announces, shooting me a sly glance. It was only a matter of time before he used this little nugget. He was probably waiting until he had a little more to drink, considering the story behind it.

With a smirk, I bring the beer to my lips, indicating I have, in fact, been carried out of a bar.

"Okay." Chloe's gaze flickers between Asher and me, able to sense he played a role in the incident. "There's obviously a story here. I need to hear it."

"Fine." I shrug, acting as if the night isn't permanently etched in my mind…and my heart. I'd never told Chloe the exact details of the night my relationship with Jessie ended. It was just easier to let everyone draw their own conclusions based on the few tidbits I provided, pretending to be too distraught to discuss it at length. By the time the dust settled, our breakup was old news.

My shoulders squared, I face her, steeling myself to get through this without giving too much away. "It was Christmas break my junior year of college. I was spending it in Connecticut with my family. Jessie was in Massachusetts. I had planned to visit him, but decided to surprise him and go early."

"Jessie? Your brother?" Lincoln asks, looking at Asher.

"Yes. They were, well…" Stammering, he rubs his hands over his shorts. "They were—"

"Engaged," I blurt out, not caring if he knows. It was years ago. Jessie doesn't matter. Or he shouldn't. But it's impossible to write him off, especially when my past and present have collided the past twenty-four hours. "Until that night." I swallow hard before my expression brightens, continuing the story. "Their parents are snowbirds who flee the cold north for the south every winter. The guys usually went down to Florida for Christmas. Well, Jessie was getting back into town that day. Asher was already back, since he was a music teacher and school had resumed. Anyway, I told Asher my plan to surprise Jessie when he got home that day."

I steal a glimpse at Asher, who stares at me furtively, brows bunched together. Not wanting to raise anyone's suspicions, I embellish the story a little.

"I had this entire scenario in my head. At first, it all *did* go according to plan. I even made Jessie the lasagna he loved, thinking he'd be hungry after traveling all day. When I heard the car pull into the driveway, I went into the dining room, taking a page from Julia Roberts' character in *Pretty Woman*. You know, when she surprised Edward wearing a tie…and that's it. Sexy, right?" My expression falls. "Until Jessie walked into the house and I could hear moans and giggles."

"Oh, Iz," Chloe exhales.

111

"He tried to apologize, promise it was just a one-time thing, but in my heart, I knew that wasn't the case, that it had probably been going on a lot longer, especially considering *she* was the one he ran to the second he landed in Boston, not me. So I stormed out of there. After getting dressed, of course. I was a mess and not thinking clearly. I was so convinced he was the perfect man for me," I lie, not wanting Chloe to poke holes in my story. It's not a complete fabrication. At one point, I *did* think he was the perfect man for me. Just not at that time. "As I tried to figure out what to do, I passed a bar."

"Which just so happened to be where my band was performing that night," Asher interjects, flashing me a smile, although it doesn't reach his eyes. I can feel his unspoken question about why I'm leaving out one rather important detail about our breakup. Maybe it's easier to put the blame on Jessie than myself. Or maybe I've told this version of the story so many times I can't be sure *what* the truth is. "Around the time we finished our first set, I looked up to see her sitting at the bar, some punk putting his hands all over her. But she was too drunk to realize what was going on."

"Not one of my finer moments."

"I knew some kind of shit had to go down for her to be there when she was supposed to be with Jessie. So I hauled her out of there before something untoward happened. Canceled the rest of our gig that night, much to the displeasure of the bar's owner, and took her to my place to sober up."

He swallows hard, and I can tell he's thinking of what happened next. How he comforted me, told me everything happens for a reason. How I took that advice to heart, thinking maybe there was a reason I'd ended up in that bar. Then how I almost kissed him, but he stopped me, telling me I was drunk and upset, that he refused to take advantage of me.

"The next morning, as he helped me nurse one of the worst hangovers of all time, I told him what happened," I explain. "To which he said…" I trail off, blinking as the words come rushing back, words I'd forgotten in the haze of everything.

"You deserve to be with someone who looks at you every day as if they won the lottery." His eyes lock with mine, a dozen emotions swirling in his mahogany depths. Sympathy. Admiration. Devotion. All things I shouldn't see from him. But I do. They were there when he uttered those words to me the first time, too, but I'd refused to acknowledge them, his rejection from the previous night still stinging. Or maybe I wasn't supposed to see them yet. Maybe it wasn't our time yet.

Is it our time now?

I quickly look away, snapping out of whatever trance Asher's mere presence places over me. "So that's how I was carried out of a bar. Who's next? It's your turn, isn't it, Chloe?"

She doesn't say anything at first, simply gapes at me. I can see the questions in her stare. I narrow my eyes, an unspoken warning not to press the topic.

"Okay then." She straightens as Lincoln sets the timer. "Never have I ever given or received a lap dance."

"Try again," I taunt, thankful for the distraction. "Already asked."

"Crap. That's right." She pulls her bottom lip between her teeth, staring into the distance as she searches the recesses of her mind for something that hasn't been said and at least one person has done. I'm glad she's in the proverbial hot seat, because my mind's coming up blank, too. All the beers I've consumed tonight certainly haven't helped.

"Ten seconds, Chloe," Lincoln warns, waving his phone in front of her.

"Okay, okay." She passes him a wry smile, the wheels spinning in her head. "Never have I ever gotten freaky in an elevator." She brings her beer to her mouth, taking a small sip, although I doubt she's actually drinking. She refuses to admit it, but Chloe's biggest fear is turning into her alcoholic mother.

I lean back into the couch, not drinking. Either does Asher. I take solace in this, the jealous monster who's flashed her teeth a few times during the game remaining in check. For now.

"Remember, we're in a bubble. Circle of trust. Blackout Club and all that. It's okay if you have."

I glance around the circle, everyone shaking their heads. "Looks like you earned a penalty round."

Chloe reaches for the dice, acting as if it's no big deal. She tosses them onto the coffee table. When they land on SUCK and TONGUE, Asher and Lincoln whistle, their devious grins floating between Chloe and me, as I suspected they would. They've been itching for us to make out all night.

Men.

"Looks like things are about to get *very* interesting." I waggle my brows.

"I suppose they are." She takes the bottle and spins it. Her sly glances at Lincoln every few seconds don't escape my notice.

As the bottle slows on Asher, I tense, the mere idea of Chloe kissing him making my stomach churn, even though there's no doubt in my mind she'd use her pass, regardless of the fact that Asher and I aren't a couple. There's still an interest there. A spark. Plus, it's girl code. Never mess around with the object of your friend's affection.

Can't the same be said for Asher, though? But in his case, it's even worse. I was once his brother's fiancée. If we were to kiss, we'd break the bro code in every way possible.

Then again, I'm pretty sure we've already broken it.

I exhale a breath when the bottle continues past him, landing on Lincoln. I whistle, passing her a playful smirk, as he casually leans back into the couch, his dark, devilish eyes trained on Chloe.

"You can use your pass if you want." His deep voice has a teasing quality to it. "I'll understand."

"Rules are rules. Plus, I'd rather save my pass for when I have to suck on Izzy's chest."

"Please don't," Asher begs, groaning. "Use your pass if you have to touch her ear, but not that. *Anything* but that." With a wink, he flashes me a boyish grin, his playfulness endearing another piece of my heart to him.

I love how one minute, he can be so sensual, so erotic, whispering how pleasurable biting my ear is. The next, he's the same Asher, whose full-bellied laughter surrounded me with comfort when I flipped over the boat we were trying to paddle in the lake. I thought he'd be pissed he got wet, but it didn't seem to bother him. Nothing ever did.

"We'll cross that bridge *if* we get to it," Chloe says, crawling toward Lincoln, straddling him, bringing her lips toward his. Apparently, this isn't going to be just a chaste kiss. "I believe the dice have spoken."

I avert my eyes, feeling like I'm snooping in on a private moment between them. If what Chloe told me earlier is true, they *haven't* kissed. They almost did, but then the lights snapped off, ruining their chance. Witnessing their first kiss feels invasive. And makes me a little jealous, wishing I were experiencing that same spark, same electricity, same excitement with Asher. There's nothing like a first kiss. The buildup. The angst. The hunger for more.

A finger brushes against my nape. I tilt my head to Asher as he rests his arm along the back of the couch, wrapping a tendril of my dark hair around a finger.

"So, when are you going to roll those dice and have the bottle land on me?" he whispers in a gruff voice. The hairs on my nape stand on end, every synapse in my body firing.

"There's no guarantee the bottle will land on you," I respond in a breathy voice. "And wouldn't it be a shame if I rolled those dice for them to land on KISS and LIPS only to spin and have to do that to Lincoln?"

"It certainly would." He licks his lips, inching closer to me, but I angle away, staying slightly out of reach, taunting and teasing him. "Then perhaps I'll just have to sabotage the bottle somehow. Use magnets so there's no way it *won't* land on me."

I give him a playful look of disapproval. "But that would be breaking the rules."

He continues to close the distance until I have nowhere to escape. "I've already broken the rules where you're concerned."

"How so?" I know the answer. I just need to hear him say it.

"I shouldn't be thinking about you this way." He traces a finger along the curve of my face, swiping my bottom lip.

"What way?"

"Like I've been starved for months, years, and have finally found a source of sustenance." He nuzzles into the crook of my neck, inhaling. "Like I've been

116

wandering the desert, and you're the mirage promising to quench this unyielding thirst."

He takes my earlobe between his teeth, nibbling. This time, the sensation is much more charged, much more electric, the idea that he's doing this because he wants to, not because the game requires him to, flaming the embers burning within.

He locks his gaze with mine. "Like I've been searching my entire life for something when it's been right in front of me all along."

A slight rustling cuts through the still night air, and he floats his attention across the coffee table. I follow his line of sight as Chloe breaks apart from Lincoln. I'd almost forgotten about them, too consumed by the spell Asher cast over me.

He pulls away, helping me back to a sitting position. Just as Chloe crawls off Lincoln's lap, Asher curves into me once more. "Regardless of whether that bottle eventually lands on me, I *will* be kissing you tonight, Isabella. That's a promise. Just like I should have let you kiss me all those years ago."

Gasping, I shoot my wide eyes to his, feigning confusion. "I don't know wha—"

"Yes, you do. And I'll be damned if I make that same mistake again."

Chapter Thirteen

"THIS GAME IS rigged," Lincoln states over Chloe's feigned moans of ecstasy, her chest heaving dramatically as I blow a light stream of air onto her finger.

"We've been waiting for one of you to spin the other all night," Asher adds.

I stand and scoot around the coffee table, smirking as I return to my position next to him on the couch.

"When you finally *do*, all you have to do is blow on her finger? I feel short-changed." He casually drapes his arm along my shoulders. This feels right, like no time at all has passed since this was a natural occurrence for us.

"Rules are rules," I sing, giving him a knowing look. "We can't just make out because you want us to, hornball." I jab him in the stomach. "If you want to see girls make out, go watch a porno."

His eyes darken as they rake over me, narrowing in on my chest. "Want to join me?"

"Maybe later." I lean closer, my lips skimming against his. He sucks in a breath, his muscles tightening. "Too bad there's no power." I abruptly pull back, pretending to be unaffected when, deep down, I don't know how much longer I can last without tossing out the rules and kissing him like I want to. "It's your turn." I hit the START button on the timer app on Lincoln's phone. "Go."

Asher's Adam's apple bobs up and down in a hard swallow as he scrubs a hand over his face, attempting to compose himself. Expelling a long breath, he tilts his head from side to side, putting his game face on.

"Never have I ever taken a sexy selfie."

"Nope!" I imitate a buzzer. "Already asked. Try again."

His head falls on the back of the couch, looking to the sky. This is my first trip to Vegas, but in the short time I've been here, I've never seen the evening sky so clear, even last night. Now that there's no other light to fight with the stars, I can appreciate their brilliance.

"Never have I ever slept with someone whose name I couldn't remember the next morning."

"Try again."

"Shit."

He squeezes his eyes shut, and I can't help but admire the concentration. It's identical to how he looks when he's in the middle of writing a song. The focus. The intensity. The passion. I can only imagine his expression when doing other…things that require concentration.

"Tick-tock," I tease.

"Never have I ever…"

"Five seconds," Lincoln taunts.

"Never have I ever…" He brings his eyes to mine, his lips parting as he struggles to come up with something. As his gaze leisurely travels down my face, his mouth curves into a sly smile.

"Four… Three…" Lincoln continues his countdown as Asher's smirk grows, his eyes lighting up with promise.

One look, and I know he has no intention of saying anything that would keep him safe from rolling those dice, regardless of the risk of the bottle landing on someone else. It's a risk he's willing to take just to have the chance to kiss me.

But I'd let him kiss me even if it's not part of our game.

"Never have I ever…," he repeats once more, his stare never leaving mine.

Chloe joins in with Lincoln's countdown, their shouts reminding me I'm not alone. I force my gaze from his, counting along with them. "Two… One…"

Swiping up the bottle, I shove it into Asher's willing hands. "Spin it, baby."

He flashes me a devious smile as he returns the bottle to the table. Remembering the order we've been doing things all evening, he retrieves the dice and rolls. When they land on KISS and LIPS, I whistle, trying to mask the butterflies flapping in my stomach.

"I'm so looking forward to watching you two make out." Chloe jabs Lincoln in the side. He wraps his arm around her shoulders, pulling her close and whispering something into her ear. Judging by the blush building on her cheeks, I doubt it was something as mundane as the weather forecast for the week.

"Time to spin, Asher," I instruct, hoping my voice drowns out the thunderous pounding of my heart.

"With pleasure." Grabbing the bottle, he places it on its side and spins.

I scoot to the edge of my seat, watching as it goes around. And around. And around. Over. And over. And over. No other spin felt like it took this long, like it's on a perpetual roulette wheel. Now I know what gamblers go through as they watch that tiny ball travel in an excruciatingly slow circle, bouncing from number to number. It could mean the difference between going home with everything they've dreamed of or walking away empty-handed.

The bottle begins to slow and my body tenses, teeth tugging at my bottom lip. My breathing increasing, the seconds stretch until it finally comes to a stop. Right in front of me. I expel my nervous energy with a laugh.

"Well then…" Asher leans toward me, scanning me up and down. "I suppose it's time we finally kiss." Indecision flashes across his expression, the see-saw of his emotions returning now that we're about to cross the proverbial point of no return. "Unless…"

Not wanting him to retreat when we've finally made it here, I clutch his cheeks, forcing him to only see me. Nothing else. "I suppose it is."

I lower myself onto my back, bringing him on top of me. The instant his body presses to mine, all the reasons we shouldn't be playing this dangerous game disappear, only raw need and desire consuming his entire being.

"I suppose it is," he repeats in a seductive tone. His lips scrape against mine, sending a delicious tremble through me. Then he nibbles on the bottom one, the unexpected jolt of pain serving to intensify the ache in my core.

"The dice say *kiss* my lips, not *bite* them."

"I know." He pulls back, his gaze locking with mine so I can see the truth in his words. "But I've imagined this for years now. I need to take advantage of it while I can, while we're still in the bubble."

I inhale a sharp breath. "*Years?*" That's all I hear, not his insinuation that once the blackout bubble vanishes, so will whatever this is. That doesn't matter right now. All that does is this moment that's been almost a decade in the making.

"Yes, Iz." He nuzzles his nose against mine, the simple gesture making my heart expand so much it's ready to combust. "Years."

"What are you waiting for?"

He smooths a tendril of hair behind my ear, the seconds agonizingly slow as his lips descend. My breaths come in pants and I brace for my first taste. So help me, nothing better interrupt this from happening, not after hours of unbearable foreplay.

When his mouth lands on mine, all the tension leaves me in a moan, my body fusing into the couch. The joining of our lips is light at first, neither one of us pushing forward. As much as I want to succumb to the swiping of his tongue against mine, his breath giving me life, his taste on my lips, I want to savor in this. It may be the only time I get to know if he's gentle or dominating, sweet or savory, desperate or hopeful. I don't want it to end. Not yet.

"God, Izzy," he groans, pressing his mouth more firmly against mine. I don't wait for him to demand entry, parting my lips for him to explore me fully, to have all of me.

His tongue swipes against mine, penetrating, devouring, needy. I tighten my hold on him, losing myself in this moment. I wasn't sure what to expect. A part of me worried he'd kiss like his brother. Jessie's kisses weren't *bad*, so to speak, but it felt…wrong. Like there was no emotion behind them. Like he was kissing me as a precursor to getting laid. Like he was going through the motions, reading an instruction manual, inserting part A into slot B, then moving on to the next set of directions.

But it's different with Asher. I can physically feel the passion brimming inside him as he takes his time exploring, discovering everything I have to offer. He consumes every inch of me with his kiss, leaving no part unaffected. I pull him closer, wrapping my legs tighter around him and pulsing. Another groan falls from his throat as he concedes to my unspoken demand, kissing me with more urgency, more ardor, more everything.

He threads his fingers into my hair, tugging, pulling, making me burn for him even more. I try not to think about the fact that I'm kissing Asher York. That we've obliterated any line between friendship and...whatever this is. That I've put him in the difficult position of betraying his brother. For brothers as close as Asher and Jessie, this *is* the ultimate betrayal.

His desperate rhythm wanes, turning into something sweeter, yet still as deep. "If I don't stop now, I'll never be able to," he murmurs against my lips, his voice raspy and heady, evidencing how much he hungers for just a taste of me. He nibbles on my lower lip one last time, which causes a nervous giggle to escape.

He gradually pulls back, helping me into a sitting position. A movement out of the corner of my eye reminds me we're not alone.

"Well, that was unexpected," I say breathlessly, trying to downplay the electric currents still pulsing through me, my skin unusually sensitive to even the light breeze caressing it.

"Hopefully in a good way." Asher wraps an arm around me, folding me into him. It's not like before when he brushed his fingers along my skin. Now his hold on me is firm and purposeful, leaving no question in my mind, in anyone's mind, that I belong to him, and vice versa. But for how much longer?

"In an amazing way." I flash him a wide smile, then quickly turn my attention back to Chloe. "Now, I believe it's Lincoln's turn. Or is it Chloe's?"

They share a look before Chloe stands. "Actually, I hate to be the one to put an end to game night, but I'm beat. It's been a long day. And tomorrow will be another long one with heading home, provided the power comes back on."

"Always the responsible one, aren't you?" I retort.

"Always."

I steal a glance at my watch to see it's only a little after midnight. Chloe's sleep schedule is almost as out of whack as mine. She often pulls all-nighters on the weekends, since that seems to be when a great deal of celebrity gossip occurs. I highly doubt she's going to her room to sleep, a suspicion that's confirmed when Lincoln offers to walk her to her room.

The second they disappear into the darkened house, an awkward silence stretches between Asher and me. He drops his arm, increasing the distance between us.

"Sorry." He runs a hand through his hair, at complete odds with the confident man whose kiss consumed me mere seconds ago. "I know this…" He trails off, licking his lips, collecting his thoughts. "Well, I guess I could have used my pass. *Should* have used my pass." A subtle laugh escapes his throat before his eyes darken, his voice coming out a potent growl. "But I've been wondering how your lips tasted for years, and I couldn't resist the temptation anymore, to hell with the consequences."

Leaning toward him, I hover my mouth over his. "And how do they taste?"

"Like the sweetest drug."

I pause before asking my next question, unsure how he'll respond. Unsure if I'm prepared for him to reject me now that it's not part of the game. "Do you want another hit?"

Groaning, his fingers circle my nape, locking me in place. "I thought you'd never ask."

I crash my lips against his, thrusting my tongue into his mouth in one quick motion. If our last kiss was an explosive culmination of years of unrequited need, this one is like a bomb going off, leveling everything in sight, just leaving him, me, and this insane craving filling my blood.

Determined hands grip my waist, yanking me on top of him. My legs fall on either side of his, a gasp sucked from my lungs when I feel how much he aches for me. I circle my hips, and he tugs me harder against him. Chest to heaving chest. Heart to racing heart. His tongue penetrates me with more frenzy, more violence, more conviction to kiss me in a way that would ruin me for all kisses to come after this one.

A fire to submit to *all* of him burns deep, the myriad of reasons this is a bad idea going up in smoke. My hands go to his chest, finding the buttons of his shirt, fumbling with them as I desperately try to rid him of his clothes. He moans when my fingers dig into his chest, nails scraping before I reach for the hem of my shirt.

"Shit. Wait." He tears away and grabs my wrists, preventing me from going any further. Conflicted eyes search mine, as if I hold the answer he so desperately needs. I suppose I do. A second passes. Then another. And another. Then he exhales, shaking his head, his shoulders falling. "We can't do this."

Those four words are the equivalent of a bucket of cold water being tossed over me. Actually, it's worse. I did the Ice Bucket Challenge all those years ago. The chill that covered me then was nothing compared to this.

I scramble off him, shooting to my feet. "We can't do this?" I shriek, hugging my arms around my stomach. "You have no problem feeling me up and practically tongue fucking my mouth, but the second I try to take things to the next level, you decide you want nothing to do with me?"

"It's not like that, Izzy." He stands, advancing toward me, but I back up, my heart squeezing, my cheeks burning with a mixture of anger and embarrassment.

"It's not like what?" I've officially reached my breaking point of the internal tug-of-war he's been playing. "You've been hot and cold all afternoon. Hell, even last night. One second, you admire me like no man in my life ever has. The next, you push me away. It's fucked with my mind."

He parts his lips to argue, but I hold up my hand, preventing him from uttering a single syllable.

"Believe me, I understand your trepidation. Don't you think I have that little ball of guilt in my stomach, too? Because I do. But this feeling in my heart is so much stronger." I draw in a deep breath, struggling to speak through the lump in my throat. "I thought it wasn't one-sided. Apparently I was wrong."

"You know that's not true." He advances, brows creased, eyes still clouded with turmoil. "I just—"

"Don't." I step back. "I don't need you to placate me with excuses. I misread the signs. I *always*—"

"You've been drinking," he interrupts.

"So have you," I accuse.

He narrows his gaze, his expression borderline condescending. At least it seems that way after his rejection. "Not as much as you. My judgment isn't compromised."

"And you think mine is?"

He shrugs. "I don't know. But I can't have that on my conscience. I refuse to take advantage of you."

I blow out a sarcastic laugh. "Sure. You had no problem 'taking advantage' of me when you were kissing me."

126

"Izzy, that's not the same thing and you know it. It was just a kiss, nothing more."

That bucket of cold water he threw on me earlier has now turned to ice, his words shattering my heart. "I see," I struggle to say.

"I didn't mean it like that. I—"

"It's okay. You don't need to explain. It *was* just a kiss." I swallow hard. "Nothing more." Doing my best to make it appear as if his rejection has little effect on me, I turn from him, heading toward the house.

"Izzy, wait."

I glance over my shoulder, his eyes pleading with me to understand. And I do. From the beginning, I knew we were playing with fire. I didn't realize how much it would burn.

"Thanks for letting us crash here. Hopefully the power comes back on soon and we'll be out of your hair." I offer him a tight-lipped smile. "Good luck. I have no doubt all your dreams will come true."

Ignoring his further pleas, I continue into the house, shining the flashlight of my phone in front of me, illuminating the path. I don't even raise my eyes to acknowledge Lincoln as he passes me on his way back outside, much to my surprise.

Safe in my room, I release a breath, falling onto the bed. I lay awake for hours, listening to the gentle sound of Asher playing guitar on the patio, holding out hope he'll come rap on my door and tell me he's willing to take a risk.

He never does.

Chapter Fourteen

I SHOULD HAVE no problem sleeping. I'm now going on almost forty-eight hours with minimal rest. While my body may be exhausted, my mind is not, too preoccupied with the wild swings of Asher's attitude toward me, culminating in his final rejection. I had plenty of warning it would end like this, given the constant push and pull. I just thought we were past that. Or I hoped we were.

In an attempt to shake off this spell Asher seems to have cast over me, I toss the covers off and step out of bed. I grab a pair of yoga pants out of my bag, slide them up my legs, adjust my tank, then walk out of my room.

The flashlight of my phone illuminating the path in front of me, I pad down the corridor, descending the stairs to the main level. The house is still, peaceful, as it should be at three in the morning.

I just wish my mind could rest, too.

As I walk toward the refrigerator to grab a bottle of water, I make out the faint sound of a piano playing a beautiful melody. Drawn to it, I'm on autopilot as my legs carry me away from the kitchen and down the hallway, the music growing louder the closer I get to the recording studio. It's haunting, the top note remaining the same despite the underlying chord changing in an even rhythm of quarter notes.

I turn off the light on my phone so as to not alert Asher, allowing his music to lead me to him, each measure sounding more heartachingly beautiful than the one preceding it. As I reach the threshold of the open door to the studio, Asher's voice carries into the hallway, stopping me in my tracks. I peer inside, the room dark, apart from a handful of candles distributed throughout. The reflection of the flames dancing on the walls makes the song even more hypnotic and heartbreaking. With no distractions typically afforded us through technology, all my attention is fully drawn to the man sitting at the piano. I listen, unable to leave if I wanted to. But I don't, not when I hear him sing of unrequited love, of never being enough, of finally giving up and moving forward. Not moving on. Not getting over it. But understanding when enough is enough.

A fitting story for the situation we find ourselves in. Or at least the situation *I* find myself in.

The intensity and passion grow as he belts out the bridge, the raspiness of his voice addicting and soul-wrenching. I know why so many females flocked to whatever bar his band played in. There's something incredibly sexy about his voice, the way his fingers caress the ivory keys of the piano with such expertise. I started playing piano when I was young myself, so I know how difficult it is. But Asher plays it as if he were born to do just that. To write music. Share his talent with the world.

The song comes to an end, his voice ringing out against the perfect acoustics of the room. I debate trying to slip away without him knowing I eavesdropped on this private moment, but there's a vulnerability in him, evidenced by the way he sits at the piano — head hung low, shoulders hunched, fingers still clinging onto the keys as if it's the only thing keeping him afloat.

"That was beautiful," I say quietly.

He shoots to his feet and whirls around, his eyes wide as they search for me in the darkness. I step out of the shadows, a candle shining a flickering light against my face.

"Izzy, what are you—"

"Is that for Fallen Grace's new album?"

He doesn't move for several long moments, simply stares at me, torn. I keep my eyes glued to his, unwavering, silently pleading with him not to push me away.

"No," he finally says, his voice low. "It's one of mine."

With a nod, I continue into the dark room. It's warmer than the rest of the house, due to the lack of ventilation and windows.

"It sounds personal," I remark, studying his expression for a reaction. But there isn't one. His face stays placid, giving nothing away, peering at me with disinterest. "Is there a story behind the lyrics?"

That gets his attention, his stance becoming rigid, the vein in his neck making an appearance, as it often does when he's at an extreme of one of his emotions. "You weren't supposed to hear that. It's still a work in progress." His mouth forming into a tight line, he scoots past me. "I should go."

I whirl around, my mouth agape. Why does he keep pushing me away? I try to understand it, try to rationalize it's because of the sticky situation between his brother and me, but my relationship with Jessie didn't stop us from being friends. In fact, it was *because* of my relationship with his brother we became such good friends. Why can't we go back to that? I have a feeling I know the reason. I need to hear him finally admit it. To me. And to himself.

"Why don't you want me?" I call out as he's about to turn the corner and disappear into the hallway. My voice echoes, the desperation in my tone surrounding me. Mocking me. Exposing me.

He stills, stopping in his tracks. His fists clenched, he shakes his head as the battle wages within, pushing him to the breaking point. He wants to face me, but he doesn't. He wants to respond, but is afraid of what his words will reveal. He wants to wrap me in his arms, but knows with every embrace, it will become more and more difficult to walk away.

"What is so wrong with me that you can't even stomach the sight of me now?" I choke out, not holding anything back. Not anymore. "So what? We kissed. Like you said, it was just a kiss. It doesn't—"

"Is that seriously what you think?" he growls, turning to face me in one swift move. My heart rate spikes, the hairs on my nape standing on end. "That it was just a kiss?"

My mouth grows dry as a jolt of adrenaline shoots through me. When he stalks toward me, I back up on instinct, the power in his gaze, in his stride, in his aura startling me.

"I—"

He clutches my cheeks, stealing my protest. "Impossible, Izzy. Fucking impossible."

"What is?" I try to look away from his stormy eyes, but I can't, a force bigger than me keeping my stare locked on his.

"That it was just a kiss. It could never be just a kiss. Not with you. Hell, I told you I'd wanted to kiss you for years. That's true. I have. I'd lost track of the number of times I went to sleep after staying up all night with

131

you and fantasized about how your lips would taste. Grew jealous whenever I had to watch my brother kiss you. God, Izzy."

His grip on me tightens as he brings his head closer to mine, a whisper between us. My breath quickens as I bask in his spicy, sweet scent, the aroma of citrus and wood wrapping me in comfort. The only comfort I've ever known.

"Every time I saw him kiss you, all I could think was how I should have been the one doing that."

I open my mouth, not wanting to bring Jessie into our bubble. That would cause it to burst, to implode into a fiery mess. He cuts me off before I can say anything.

"Every time I saw him place his hand on your leg and run his finger along your exposed flesh, all I could think about was how cavalier he was about it. How he should have appreciated you for the fucking gift you were."

He loosens his hold on my face, one hand going to my nape, the other sliding down my frame. When he lifts the hem of my tank top and caresses the exposed flesh, a shiver runs through my body.

"And every time I said good night to you, only for you to go to bed, to *his* bed..." His nostrils flare, a tick in his jaw. "All I could think about was that it should have been *my* bed. *My* arms that held you. *My* body that worshipped yours."

No words come. How can I respond? Tell him I always craved his company but assumed he'd never be interested in me, not when so many girls who were more mature and experienced than me sought him out? That every time I heard him perform a new song, a part of me wished he were singing about me?

That the real reason I ended things with Jessie was because I realized I'd also fallen in love with Asher?

"I don't have the same competitive nature as my brother," he continues when I don't say anything. "I don't need to prove I can be the best at everything I do. I never wanted to graduate at the top of my class. Be class president. Run the world. The only person I care about being better than is the person I am today." He chuckles, a momentary break in the tension. "Although, after tonight, you could probably argue I haven't exactly been a good person."

My chest squeezes at the reminder of the position I put him in. I told myself I wouldn't allow him to put his relationship with his brother at risk. But that was before I was cast under his spell again. Before I was reminded of why I'd allowed him to possess a piece of my heart. Before I had a taste of him after years of fantasizing. It's left me desperate for more.

"I've never wanted something he had, never wanted to be him." He returns his hands to my face, leaning toward me. "Until you." His hold on me tightens as he erases the last bit of space between us, sealing my mouth with his.

He leaves me no room to protest, his kiss touching every part of me, stealing my breath, invading my soul as I succumb to what this man does to me with just a simple meeting of our mouths. But nothing with us has ever been simple. His kiss isn't, either. In it is a piece of his heart. And mine. Fusing together in this beautiful connection most people search for their entire lives.

I wrap my arms around his broad shoulders, curving into him, even a heartbeat between our bodies too much space. He moans, a surge of electricity reawakening me. His hands roam my body, his sensual touch making me feel wanted. Not like so many other men who just wanted to cop a quick feel of my chest before pulling out their dick. But not Asher. Hell, he hasn't even brushed a single finger against my breasts, which only increases my need, moisture pooling between my thighs at the thought.

A hand grips my hip, and he backs me across the room until my legs hit the baby grand piano. Grasping my ass, he lifts me onto the surface with ease, as if I weigh no more than a speck of dust. I try to stay in shape, but I'm not a waif. My five-seven frame is leggy, my Mexican heritage giving me an ample chest and curvy hips.

When I part my thighs and pull his body between them, he groans, his lips leaving mine for the first time. A man starved, he runs his tongue along my jawline, the scruff of his unshaven face causing a delicious ache to settle in my core. I've never been so aroused, so ready to toss aside reason for one moment of ecstasy.

"Fuck, Izzy," he growls as I tighten the grip my legs have around his waist. When his erection throbs against me, I whimper, my body trembling from the sensation of him through our fully clothed bodies. If I'm on the cusp of coming undone from this, I can only imagine what it'll be like when it's flesh against flesh. I refuse to wait any longer to find out.

I fist his shirt in my hand, tugging him into me, my fingers fumbling for the buttons. He straightens, abruptly stepping back. My heart drops to the pit of my stomach as my eyes lock with his. I swallow hard, unsure if I can handle him rejecting me yet again.

Then a lazy smirk crawls across his lips as he leisurely unfastens the top button of his shirt, making a show of it. My shoulders falling out of relief, I place my hands behind me on the piano, sucking in my bottom lip.

"If you're trying to audition for one of those all-male reviews, I'll have you know they're quick with taking off their shirts. Hell, most of the time they're not wearing a shirt at all."

He pauses, mid-unbutton, a single brow cocked. "Is that right?"

"That's right."

"Well then…" He smiles deviously. "Maybe you should give me a lesson."

"In what?" I straighten, my voice rising in pitch. "Stripping?"

His eyes flicker with mischief as he closes the distance between us, leering at me in a way that strips me bare. In the most tantalizing of ways. "Didn't you say Bernadette made you all go to striptease and pole dance lessons?"

"She did, but…"

He leans into me and his teeth capture my earlobe, tugging on it, erasing any objection from my mind. I'll do whatever he asks if it means I'll be rewarded with his tongue on me. On every inch of me.

"Please, Izzy. Dance for me. Just like you used to whenever our band played 'Amante'."

All it takes is hearing the title of one of his earlier songs to be transported back to my college days. To my roommate dragging me to a club where a hot, local band was playing. To falling in love with the music and making a point of returning week after week. To being unable to stop from swaying my hips whenever they played that particular song, a sensual, Latin-inspired rhythm that spoke to me the first time I heard the opening measures.

He extends a hand to me. Does the idea of stripping for Asher turn me on? Hell yes. But to this song? One I always felt he wrote for me after he noticed me in the audience that first night. After his earlier confession

135

that he's been wanting to kiss me for years, it's not that far out of the realm of possibility.

My eyes focused on his dark pools, I place my hand in his. In one quick movement, he pulls me off the piano, spinning me around so my back is pressed against his front. The sudden motion steals my breath, a gasp escaping. My surprise turns into a burning need when he sensually circles his hips against me.

"When I wrote it, I always imagined you stripping to it. Even though I didn't even know your name." He runs a calloused hand along my collarbone before easing his way up to my throat, wrapping his fingers around it. I crane my head, my breath coming in pants, a surge of hunger filling me from his possessive hold. His mouth skates near my earlobe, teeth nipping at my flesh. "Never thought that fantasy would come true."

He drops his hold on me, stepping back. I remain still, a bundle of sensation. How the hell did we get here? How did I go from wanting to clear my head to considering giving Asher a striptease in the span of mere minutes? As is always the case with us, some things just can't be explained.

The opening lines sound from Asher's cell phone, and I close my eyes. My body still tingling, I'm on the brink of unraveling, a slave to Asher's touch. And I'll do whatever it takes to have his touch again.

I glance over my shoulder, flashing him a seductive smile. My tongue skates across my bottom lip in an elaborate show, as if I'm about to feast on the finest of delicacies. That's exactly what this man is. Six-foot-two. Broad shoulders. Defined muscles. And that perfect V disappearing into the waistband of his shorts. I could overindulge on him for hours and still not get my fill.

With slow motions, I face him, swaying my hips in time with the music as I advance toward him. My hands resting against the hard planes of his tattooed-covered chest, I push him into a chair in the corner of the room. He doesn't protest, simply obeys my unspoken command, his eyes never leaving mine.

I take several steps back, increasing the distance between us. One of the things I'd learned in my striptease lessons is that it's important not to give it all away at first. Stay out of reach. Make them want you. Beg for you. That's what I do.

The music comes to an abrupt stop, and I dart my eyes to Asher.

"I'm going to start the song over." There's a flash in his gaze. A heat. A warning. "If this is the only time I'll ever experience this, I need to milk it for every damn second. Every chord. Every eighth note. I need it all."

"God, I love a man who can talk music to me," I joke in a sensual tone, although my words hold a great deal of truth. Music has always been a turn-on for me. And a man who plays a musical instrument? One who appreciates the patience and practice essential to master it? That's the kind of man I want to be with.

"Well, you can blow my horn any day, baby."

I giggle, then quickly cover my mouth. "Sorry."

"What are you sorry about? I love your laugh."

"I know. It's just… I'm supposed to be doing this whole seductive temptress act here."

"Well, tempt away." He starts the song again before setting his phone on a nearby table, freeing his hands.

I close my eyes, taking a moment to allow the provocative rhythm to invade my soul as it did all those years ago when I couldn't help but move with the melody. It has a more mature sound now, evidence he must have re-recorded it. When his voice sings about

137

spotting a beautiful woman in a bar who ends up infiltrating his every thought, it's deeper, more raspy, more soulful. The way Asher is today.

Shaking off my nerves, I fix my expression in front of me, emboldened by the fire I can make out in Asher's gaze. The few flickering candles create the perfect ambience for this, the darkness a blanket protecting me, allowing me to pretend I'm all alone, dancing for no one. It's not the first time I've danced to this song. This is no different from dancing to it when his band played it during my college days.

Except this time, I'll end up naked when the dance is over.

I sway my hips, subtly at first, allowing my soul to feel the music. Muscle memory kicks in, my body forgetting about the years that have passed since I've danced. I move with more confidence, tuning everything else out as I lose myself in the erotic sound of Asher's voice filling the room.

Approaching him, I run a lithe finger along his chest and collarbone before moving behind his chair. He attempts to glance over his shoulder, but I force his head forward. When I scrape my nails against his firm chest from behind, he throws his head back, a moan escaping his lips. Carnal. Wanton. Igniting.

As desperate as I am to keep feeling the warmth of his body on my fingertips, I remove my hands and circle to the front of his chair. I can see the raw need emanating from every pore, the fire in his eyes enough to light all of Las Vegas.

He reaches out, gripping my hip, pulling me closer. Giving him a playful look of admonishment, I take his hand, removing it. "No touching," I murmur breathlessly.

"God, you're going to kill me," he groans as I straddle him, pulsing my hips against his waist. I jut out my chest, leaning closer so I'm a breath away.

His body tightens beneath me in all the right places, giving me an added boost of confidence, knowing I do this to him. That the sight and feel of me, even fully clothed, pushes him to the point of oblivion. There's nothing so addictive. I now understand why some girls love stripping. I'd rolled my eyes when the woman teaching our class told us how powerful it made her feel, even when she felt she was losing control of everything else in her life. But the second she stepped into the club, she'd felt in charge, in control.

I hoist myself higher, my long, dark hair forming a curtain around us as I continue teasing and torturing. The frustration builds in his expression, and I can tell it's taking every ounce of resolve he possesses not to touch me, not to grip my hips or squeeze my ass as he takes charge of my seduction.

My lips skim against his, and he cranes his head toward mine, chasing my kiss, but I don't allow him to capture it just yet. Desperation blooms and grows, and I know he won't be able to hold off much longer. I don't think I will, either, the restraint I've had to exhibit until this point nearly making me combust.

Playfully waggling my brows, I pull back, climbing off him in measured movements. My eyes locked on his, I slip my fingers into the waistband of my yoga pants, teasing him by exposing a flash of skin on my hip before retreating, dancing around him once more. When he groans, I inwardly smile. I've been with my fair share of men over the past several years. Not one of them had ever been so unabashedly shameless in his need for me. So many men, at least in New York, have a "take it or leave it" attitude, thinking if it doesn't work out, there's always someone else who'd give them a piece of ass. But Asher has no qualms about showing me just how much he needs me.

Moving in front of him, I turn around, facing away. I pause for a beat, drawing in a breath. Once I do this, there's no going back. Then again, there was no going back the second we kissed. We both knew what we were getting into, yet did it anyway.

Hooking my fingers into my waistband, I slowly slide my pants down my legs, praying those years of ballet classes will pay off and keep me upright. I lean over, my legs remaining straight as I tease Asher, my ass dangling in front of him like a delicious treat.

A hiss echoes in the room. "You're killing me, Izzy." The unquenchable thirst in his voice nearly pushes me over the edge. I don't want to rush this. Don't want this to end.

Straightening, I step out of my yoga pants, sauntering back up to him, clad only in my tank top and panties. When I draw near this time, he cups my ass, tugging me toward him.

"Tsk, tsk, tsk." I curve into him, my lips hovering over his. "Didn't I already have to warn you once about touching?"

"I've never been one to listen to directions. You should know that about me."

"I do. But you were the one who asked me to strip."

"I changed my mind." He brings a hand to the back of my neck, his hold firm, unwavering, demanding. "If I don't have you right now, I'll lose my fucking head." He crushes his mouth against mine, his kiss stealing my breath with its ferocity. He thrusts his tongue past my lips, his loss of all control like the most addictive drug. Growing dizzy from the kiss, I manage to push away, panting.

"I can't deprive you of your fantasy."

"Don't you realize? *You* are my fantasy." This time when he kisses me, it's not as frenzied, but still brimming with want. Maybe more so. It's slower. Heavier. Sharper.

His hands go beneath my tank, skimming against my abdomen, deliberately making their way up to my chest. When he cups my breasts, I succumb to his touch, needing more. The tips of his fingers skim against my nipples, which harden instantly, eliciting a moan.

"Take off your top," Asher murmurs against my lips before burying his head in the crook of my neck, licking and sucking before pulling back.

Unable to deny him anything, I grab the hem of my shirt, yanking it over my head in one quick move, tossing it onto the floor.

He takes a minute to look at me. But unlike every other guy I've been with in the past, he doesn't stare at my chest. Instead, his eyes stay on mine. A finger traces the curve of my face before he threads his fingers through my hair, drawing my lips back to his.

"You are so fucking beautiful, Isabella." He eliminates the last breath between our mouths, but I retreat.

"I don't want to give it all up so soon. Not when you were hoping to get the most out of this seduction."

"Trust me. I have."

"How? I only danced for half a song."

He clutches my cheeks with both hands. "You seduced me the first time I saw you. Maybe not physically, but in here." He releases me, tapping the side of his head. His Adam's apple bobs up and down when he brings that same hand to his heart. "And here. The more time I spent with you, the more I got to know

141

you, the more you seduced my soul." He grips my nape, pulling me back toward him. "Every fiber of my being."

His words are so choked with emotion, my brain refuses to fire. What can I say to that? A voice inside tells me he doesn't mean it, that this is just part of *his* seduction. After all, he *is* a writer. A musician. A poet. These words are second nature for him, as easy and natural as jotting down his grocery list. But I can't ignore the truth in his eyes. It's vibrant. Real. Spellbinding. Even the most practiced of actors couldn't fake that.

"So, to address your concerns, you needn't feel like you're short-changing me." He nibbles on my lower lip. A moan rattles from my throat at the perfect contact. "I've been able to enjoy a decade worth of your dance of seduction. Now I can finally join you. Let me join you."

I slam my lips to his, pressing my body as far into his as possible, needing to feel every strained muscle, every hard surface, every drum of his heart that only beats for me.

He runs his hands along the lines of my stomach, brushing the swell of my breasts before retreating once more. I don't want him to retreat. Only want him to push forward. Grabbing his hands, I press them against my chest, throwing my head back when he rolls my nipples between his thumb and forefinger.

He leaves a trail of desperate kisses along my jawline, his scruff rough but achingly pleasurable as it scrapes against my skin. Cupping my breasts tighter, he lowers his mouth. I curve back as best I can in our awkward position, my breathing increasing at the promise of feeling his lips on me.

Suddenly, I'm lifted, and I fling my eyes open. "Hold on," he rasps.

I do as he commands, tightening my grip around his neck as he transitions me into a cradle carry. Shoving his phone into his pocket, he walks with purposeful strides out of the studio, practically running up the stairs and into my bedroom, kicking the door shut behind him. I want to ask why he didn't take me back to his room, but before I have a chance to worry about that, he places me onto the mattress, slithering up my frame.

A whimper falls from my throat when his tongue traces delicate circles around my belly button. The touch is light, but hits me so deep, the way he worships me pushing my body higher and higher.

"Please, Asher," I beg, gripping the sheets as I writhe below him.

He cranes his head up, a salacious smirk forming on his lips. "Something I can help you with?"

Chest heaving, I clutch his face in my hands, tugging him toward me. "If I don't feel you in the next two seconds, I'm going to get myself off. And I'd much rather *you* do that."

"Now *that* sounds fucking hot." He seals his mouth over mine, his tongue sweeping against mine as he caresses the contours of my frame, inching farther south. When a finger swipes under the material of my panties, I circle my legs around his waist, pulsing, needing, wanting.

"Please." My word comes out a desperate plea, my eyes rolling into the back of my head as his hand grows closer and closer to my center.

Breaking our kiss, he hooks his fingers into the band of my panties. Pausing, his eyes lock with mine, giving me one last chance to back out. When I nod, he crushes his lips to mine, his kiss too short for my liking. Then again, I get the feeling his kisses will always seem too short. The way they seem to devour my soul has increased my appetite for him to a nearly incomprehensible level. I can take and take and take, yet fear I'll always need more of him.

His motions are slow as he lowers my panties down my legs, his eyes not breaking from mine, as if waiting for me to change course. But I can't. Tonight was the perfect storm. The canceled flight. The invitation to stay here. The blackout. All the pieces snapped into place for this to happen. There's no reason to deprive ourselves of this.

After tossing my panties onto the floor, he runs a hand up my leg, his tongue following. I throw my head back, the ecstasy from his soft touch more than I can handle. With every inch, my core tightens in promise of what's to come. When a finger ghosts against my center, I moan, my pulse skyrocketing.

"God, you're so wet."

"Because you're driving me crazy. I told you I needed to get off."

"Well then," he begins coyly. "Allow me the...pleasure." He waggles his brows, then brings his mouth to me, his tongue lapping up my juices.

I melt into the mattress, all the tension rolling off my body at how expertly he tastes me, then inserts a finger, stretching and exploring. "I believe the pleasure is all mine," I murmur as if having an out-of-body experience.

"Oh no, baby. This is all mine."

"Yours..." I run my hand through his locks as he inserts another finger, pushing me higher and higher, my body flooding with warmth in places I didn't even think existed. I've never felt so full. So complete. So beautiful.

"All mine," he growls, picking up speed.

It takes no time at all for me to succumb to his ministrations, the combination of his erotic touch and the amount of time since I've been with a man sending me over the edge. Lights flash before my eyes, despite the darkness shrouding the room, my body convulsing as one of the most intense orgasms I've experienced rolls through me. But that doesn't make Asher stop. He keeps licking, tasting, devouring, wanting every last drop, every last shake, every last tremor until I have nothing left to give, my cries echoing into the Las Vegas night through the open window in my bedroom.

Sated, I flutter my eyes open, meeting Asher's lazy smile that's coated in my desire. "I hope that was as enjoyable for you as it was for me."

Cheeks clutched in my hands, I drag him toward me, kissing him fully, tasting me and him in one incredibly erotic combination. "I need you inside me," I murmur, nibbling on his lower lip.

"And I need to be inside you." His expression falls. "But I don't have any condoms. I wasn't exactly planning on this happening, so I—"

"It's okay. I'm on the pill. I trust you."

Asher was never the type to sleep around. Granted, it's been years since we've seen each other. In some respects, he's not the same Asher. I don't think he's changed *that* much.

"Are you sure? I don't want you to feel like you have to if you're not comfortable without protection."

I flip him onto his back in one swift move. His eyes flame before darkening. I sensually grind my hips against his, my hair falling around us.

"I need you." I reach down, palming the erection straining to be released. "And I can feel how much you need me. I want this, Asher. More than I've wanted anything I can remember in years." I bring my lips to his, skimming them. "I want *you*."

He delicately pushes a curl out of my eyes. I expect him to treat me to a beautiful kiss. Instead, his gaze becomes clouded with lust as he grips my hair forcefully, passion surging through me. "And I want you." He yanks my head to the side, his teeth clamping onto my neck. I release a noiseless gasp. I didn't think this kind of pleasure was possible. "So fucking much."

"Then have me."

With a growl, he flips me onto my back, climbing off me to undress. A sliver of moonlight illuminates him as he shrugs his shirt off his shoulders, revealing even more ink on his back. He's not fully covered, but the few tattoos that spread from his shoulder blades onto his arms are tasteful. They're the perfect accent to his broad shoulders, not obscuring his sculpted pecs or defined abs.

His eyes remain steady on mine as he unbuttons his shorts and pushes them down his legs, his arousal springing free. It takes every ounce of resolve I possess not to compare Jessie to Asher. One thing is certain. There is one area where Jessie will never be able to outshine his brother. While Jessie was pretty well-endowed, and the inexperienced girl I was when we first had sex thought he used it quite well, it's no match for Asher.

He crawls onto the bed, slithering up my body. When he settles between my thighs, I enclose my legs around his waist, the feel of flesh against flesh causing my stomach to clench in anticipation.

Pulling back, he lifts his erection to me, spreading my wetness around. Neither one of us looks away as he pushes into me, inch by incredible inch, stretching and filling before retreating, then sliding back in again. He continues acclimating my body to his, every motion deliberately sensual, giving me a taste of how amazing it could be before pulling back.

I dig my hands into his scalp, tugging him against me, chest to chest, heart to heart. I cover his mouth with mine, tightening my hold around his waist, matching his rhythm. He moans, the vibration in his chest hitting the deepest parts of my soul.

I rake my nails up his back and he tears his lips from mine, arching into the contact, his chest heaving, sweat forming on his brow. "You're driving me fucking crazy."

I crane toward him, taking his earlobe between my teeth. "That's the point."

With a groan, he increases his sensual rhythm, each thrust deeper and more fulfilling. I fall back onto the mattress as his lips kiss every part of me he can get to. My mouth. My neck. My chest. His frenzied hands explore every inch of my body, squeezing and bruising. When his finger rubs against my clit, I moan, my breathing growing ragged.

"I want you to come again."

I'm about to tell him I don't think I can, that it's never happened, when that familiar tingling sensation bubbles deep inside, becoming brighter and stronger until I scream out, waves of mind-erasing pleasure washing over me.

An animalistic growl rips from Asher's lungs, the sensual, seductive lover turning into a man obsessed, desperate, hungry. He brings my legs onto his shoulders, increasing his rhythm to an almost punishing level as he drives into me, harder, deeper, faster, eyes dark, frantic, pained.

He stills, emitting a strangled cry as his warmth spreads through me, his motions jerky. Tremors overtake him and he releases his hold on my legs, allowing them to fall to the mattress before he covers my body with his. Our labored breathing fills the room, stark against the silence, which is even more pronounced due to the lack of power.

"Damn," he breathes, nuzzling my chest. "I knew sex with you would be good. I just never could have imagined it would be so…electric."

I smirk. "You imagined?"

He lifts his eyes to mine, a salacious grin crossing his mouth. "You better believe it. Let's just say, for quite a few years, you were the leading lady of my spank bank."

With a laugh, I push him off me. "Gross." I attempt to scoot away, but he wraps an arm around my waist, pulling me back into him, thwarting my lackluster escape plan. When he brushes my hair over my shoulder and peppers soft kisses along my shoulder blades, I can't help but melt into him.

"You can't tell me you've never thought of someone else when you touched yourself."

"Maybe," I muse.

He nuzzles his nose into my neck. "And who would that lucky bastard be?"

I shift my position, turning to face him. "What would you say if I told you I've thought of you?"

Impassioned, he covers my mouth with his, his kiss brief but still full. "I'd say that's one of the hottest things I've heard in a long time." He grabs my knee, hooking my leg over his waist, thrusting to demonstrate his reawakening arousal. "And when was this?"

Leaning toward him, I scrape my teeth along his pec. "This morning." My answer comes out breathy. "I get really horny first thing in the morning."

He groans, smashing my body against his, his arms enveloping me. "You're going to be my undoing. Do you know that?"

"That's what I'm hoping for."

Chapter Fifteen

THE SOFT TICKLE of chest hair against my back stirs me from a restful sleep. One of the most restful nights I've had in a while. I exhale a contented sigh, not wanting to open my eyes, able to sense the sun is already bathing the room in light. I don't want it to be day. Not yet. Not when that means I'll have to come to terms with what Asher and I did last night.

He tightens his arm around my waist, pulling me into his body, a raspy moan reverberating through his chest. "Mmm." He subtly thrusts against me, jumpstarting my libido, as if she needs any help. Just being near this man skyrockets my sex drive. "I can get used to waking up like this."

"What? With some naked chick in your bed?"

"Not just any naked chick." His hand travels along my stomach, making the laborious journey south. I adjust my legs, parting them, an unspoken invitation to continue his exploration of my body. "Only you. I can get used to waking up next to you."

When he toys with my folds, I succumb to his touch, ignoring the voice of reason telling me to put a stop to this, to find out what time it is, if the power's come back on. By the whirring fan kicking on from the central air and heating system, I surmise it is. I don't want to do anything to interrupt this moment.

"I can get used to this, too," I whimper as he inserts a finger, then another, massaging me in the most delicious of ways.

He pulses against me, and I part my thighs even more, allowing him better access. "Prop your leg up with your foot," he orders. "With your knee bent."

I do as he asks, which spreads my legs wider. He grips the underside of my thigh, pulling it to the other side of his body, leaving me sprawled out and at the mercy of his fingers.

"God, Izzy…" He scrapes his teeth along my neck, the pleasurable pain almost more than I can bear. "I need you one more time."

I moan, lost in the sensation, unable to form a single coherent thought.

"Do you want me?" He pushes his finger deeper, tantalizing and teasing. I couldn't tell him no if I wanted to, my mind devoid of reason.

"Y-yes."

"I was hoping you'd say that." He withdraws his fingers, the lack of his touch causing an unwelcome chill to wash over me. But before I can beg for more, his length thrusts against me from behind, sliding into me.

We exhale simultaneously and he pauses, filling me before retreating, continuing his same sensual motion. Over. And over. And over. My jaw falls slack, a noiseless whimper escaping at the utter bliss invading me. Last night was incredible. I'd never been with any man as selfless and passionate as Asher. But this position, lying on my side with my back to his front, my leg propped up, he's able to hit parts of me no other man ever has.

"Asher," I manage to say, my veins throbbing with the electric current burning through me. "I don't—"

151

"Touch yourself," he orders gruffly, cutting me off. "I want to feel your pussy clench around me."

A slave to his demand, I lower my hand between my legs, toying with my clit. My teeth clench with the unmatched desire seizing me. The idea of touching myself while Asher fucks me is all I need to come undone, my world crumbling into a thousand pieces of the most brilliant light.

"Yes," he hisses. "Like that." He picks up his pace, his hand squeezing my thigh, spreading me more, his punishing grip only serving to increase my pleasure. "So. Damn. Good." Each word is punctured with another thrust until he climaxes, a suppressed roar ripping through the room.

The tremors overtaking his body match my own in intensity. I can't remember sex ever being like this. I'm not naïve by any stretch of the imagination. I've had my fair share of a variety of relationships, from committed to one-night stands and everything in between. But it's never been like this. This powerful. This inspiring. This explosive. I wonder if Asher feels the same way. By the way he struggles to catch his breath, the way his heart pounds against my back, the way he seems to be speechless, I imagine he probably does.

A ringtone cuts through our heavy breaths, and I sigh at the confirmation that the blackout is over. I glance at my watch on the nightstand to see it's after nine. As much as I'd love to stay in this bed all day, I need to pack my things and get to the airport. I have to get home today.

"Aren't you going to answer that?" I ask when Asher doesn't make any move.

"I wasn't planning on it. I'd hoped to stay right here with my cock inside you as long as I can. Then when my happy warrior snaps to attention, I'll already be in position."

I laugh, wiggling my butt against him as the ringing stops. "Well, maybe I should help him along."

"He's a little spent right now, but I'm sure he can be coaxed into playing again very soon." He nips at my shoulder blade. "Maybe in the shower."

"Mmm. I can get on board with that."

When his phone rings again, he groans.

"You should get that. Whoever it is must have an important reason to try you twice in a row."

"They should know better than to call me in the morning."

"True." I shimmy away as he slides out of me. Facing him, I feather my lips against his. "But I'll make you a deal. You answer your phone, then come join me in the shower where you can wash every inch of me clean. And I do mean every..." I drag my tongue along his jawline. "Single." I dig my fingers into his chest. "Inch." My mouth covers his before I scoot off the bed and pad toward the bathroom.

Just before I disappear behind the door, I glance over my shoulder, giving myself a mental high-five when I see his erection spring back to life.

Chapter Sixteen

"**Y**OU'RE INSATIABLE, IZZY," Asher struggles to say, our breathing even more ragged after the strenuous effort it takes to have sex in a shower. It's not as easy as romance novels make it seem. You need to be in damn good shape to keep your body upright. Thankfully, Asher is in amazing shape, his flexing muscles able to support my sated frame with ease.

"You're not so bad yourself," I reply, kissing him, my skin still tingling.

He practically has to peel my legs from around his waist as he steps away, helping me find my footing. My balance is a little unsteady from the amount of sex we've had the last several hours. In the past six months, I don't think I've had sex the number of times I have these past six hours. A girl could get used to this.

After rinsing off one last time, he places a soft kiss on my forehead. "I'll let you finish showering on your own."

"Oh really?" I pout dramatically. "You really want to leave this?" I step under the stream, allowing it to cascade over my breasts.

Asher's in front of me in a heartbeat, yanking my body against his. He seals his mouth over mine, water falling over him, me, and our kiss before he pulls away, chest heaving. "I don't want to leave you, but if I don't walk away now, I won't be able to keep my hands off you. Then I'll have to kidnap you and keep you here forever."

"You won't hear any complaints from me."

"Me, either." Leaving me with a delicate kiss on my temple, he opens the shower door and grabs a towel, securing it around his waist.

God, there's nothing sexier than Asher York wearing only a towel, droplets of water gleaming on his body.

I steal a glance as he pauses in front of the long vanity, briefly leaning his arms against the counter. He closes his eyes, blowing out a long breath. It's a fleeting expression of remorse, but it still hits me, reminds me of the reality of what we've done.

Once he walks out of the bathroom, I finish showering as quickly as possible. I don't have much time left before I need to get to the airport to catch my flight. When I checked the status, it showed on time, much to my surprise.

As I towel off my hair, Asher reappears in the doorway of the bathroom, dressed in a pair of jeans and t-shirt. "Hey." He crosses his arms in front of his chest, leaning on the doorjamb.

"Hey."

"So, I need to tell you something, but I don't want you to freak out."

"Okay…" My response is drawn-out as I straighten my spine, re-securing the towel wrapped around my body.

He pushes off the wall, his eyes averted. From this alone, I can sense I'm not going to like what he's about to say. He runs his hands through his hair that's still damp from our sex-filled shower. On a long exhale, he slowly lifts his gaze to meet mine.

"That was Jessie on the phone."

My pulse increases slightly. Since I stepped foot into the studio last night, I haven't thought of Jessie more than a fleeting comparison in size. Based on the expression on Asher's face, I have a feeling that's about to end.

"And?" I ask, my voice trembling.

He doesn't say anything right away, simply stares at me. Then he sighs. "He's downstairs."

"What?"

My heart plummets to the pit of my stomach, frantic eyes searching his for an indication that this is a joke. That this isn't real. But all I see is the same honesty I always have from Asher. He wouldn't lie to me, not about this.

"How?" I push past him, darting toward my suitcase. I hastily throw all my items back into it, a need to get out of this house overtaking me. "Do you think he knows?"

"Of course not. Pretty sure he would have greeted me with a broken nose instead of a hug."

"Then why—"

He places his hands on my biceps in an attempt to placate me, but nothing can. This all just got real. A little too real. I knew what I was getting into last night. Knew the ramifications, but ignored them. The blackout bubble seduced me into thinking we wouldn't suffer the consequences of our actions. At least not anytime soon. For once, I chose to live in the moment. And now we'll both have to pay the price.

"He heard about the blackout and came out to check on me."

"From Boston? How did he get a flight if the airport just reopened?"

He licks his lips, his gaze steady, expression calm. "Because he doesn't live in Boston anymore." He swallows hard. "He lives in Los Angeles. He's…" He hesitates. "He's my manager."

My body freezes, his words a punch to the gut. "Your manager?" I squeak out, blindsided.

Granted, I never asked who his manager was, or if he even had one, but considering my history with Jessie, you'd think Asher would have mentioned that little tidbit of information. It's not just a familial relationship I'm dealing with here. Asher and Jessie have a professional relationship, too. It's like learning the guy I just had amazing sex with is my ex's new boss. But it's worse with us, because I should have known better. Now, there's so much more at stake than I ever could have imagined.

"Yes." He doesn't embellish any further, but he doesn't need to. It makes sense. Jessie was a business major, a natural salesman. He could charm the squirrels out of the trees in the dead of winter, even though they knew it was their only means of protection against the elements. Not to mention, right after college, Jessie worked as a client specialist for a talent agency in Boston. He understands the business side of the music industry. There's no one else Asher would trust with his career. It was always their plan.

I shake off his touch, shrinking into myself. "Why didn't you tell me?"

"It didn't seem like it mattered."

"Didn't seem like it mattered?" I repeat, my voice rising in pitch. I quickly lower it, unsure where Jessie is. For all I know, he could be eavesdropping outside the door. "It matters. It matters a lot. So… What? You let Jessie in and then came up to fuck me one last time before dropping this bomb?" My disbelief at this situation growing, I grab the first pair of pants I find in

157

my disheveled suitcase and yank them on, not caring I'm not wearing any underwear.

"It's not like that, Iz. I'm as surprised as you are. I bought us a little time and have him in the studio, listening to some demos I've written for a solo album I have in the works."

I slow my motions, finding solace in the fact that Jessie's locked away in the opposite end of the house. Then memories from last night float back and my eyes widen.

"Asher! My pants and tank top are in there! They have my perfume all over them. The same perfume I wore back in college. The same perfume he bought me repeatedly. If he picks them up and—"

"Relax," he soothes, running his hands down my arms. "I grabbed them and brought them back up here before letting him in." He nods at the pants I just tugged on. "You're wearing them."

"That still doesn't make this okay." I push out of his hold, grabbing a bra and slipping it on, facing away from Asher. It's not like he hasn't seen me naked. For the past several hours, that's the *only* way he's seen me. But I feel exposed, especially now that we've been propelled into the real world, facing the consequences of sleeping together. After tugging on a shirt, I add, "You should have told me."

"Would that have changed anything?"

I whirl around to face him, my mouth agape. How do I answer that? *Would* it have changed anything? Would I have wanted Asher any less than I did last night?

When he reaches for my face and brushes his fingers against my skin, I can't help but melt into the contact. One touch is all I need to reassure me that his intentions were noble, even if the outcome was less than desirable.

Maybe I'm just overreacting. Did his omission really do any harm? I can't see how.

"I understand I should have mentioned it. But I didn't want to burst our bubble. Wanted to prevent you from enduring any heartache." He brings his lips toward mine, and I sigh at the promise of his kiss. "Just like I hoped to do all those years ago."

I melt into him, digging my hands into his hair, his words wrapping around me like a blanket. But as the meaning in his statement sank in, I stiffen, pushing against him.

"What did you say?"

Disoriented, he blinks repeatedly. This time, *he's* at a loss for words. "I—"

"What heartache did you want to prevent all those years ago?" I step back, eyeing him with suspicion, a knot tightening in my stomach.

"I...," he stammers, his breathing quickening.

"What heartache did you want to prevent?" I ask again through clenched teeth, my temper flaming. He doesn't say anything. He doesn't have to. The answer is etched in the worry lines on his face. In his pleading eyes. In the hard bob of his Adam's apple.

I back up. It makes perfect sense. I always wondered why Asher argued vehemently against my decision to surprise Jessie. Now I know why.

"Oh, my god. You knew. That's what you mean, right? When you said you hoped to prevent my heartache, you're talking about that night, aren't you?"

Again, he remains silent. What *is* there to say?

"How could you keep that from me? You knew what I was walking into, yet—"

"No." He darts his eyes to mine, that vein in his neck throbbing. His fists clench, every muscle in his body vibrating with a passion I've yet to see in another

159

person. Even him. "I had no idea what you were walking into."

"But—"

"Maybe you've forgotten, because the story you told last night left out quite a few things."

"I didn't think it was necessary to go into all the gory details."

"Really?" Defensive, he folds his arms across his chest. "Is that why Chloe didn't even seem to know what happened? Why she appeared just as interested in the story as someone who'd never heard it? Because you didn't think it was necessary to go into 'all the gory details' with one of your dearest friends when it happened? Don't you always say that keeping the truth is as bad as lying?"

"That's not the same, and you know it. The details didn't involve Chloe."

What can I say to him? That the reason I left out so many details was because of what I feared it would finally reveal. That the real reason I ran out on Jessie wasn't because he sought comfort in another woman's embrace. After all, I did play a part in pushing him there. It was because, as I sat waiting for him, I found myself staring at a photo of Asher and me together, my mother's words ringing around me.

"How will I know if he owns my heart?"

"You'll just…know."

"How?"

"You'll see it in his eyes. You'll see a piece of yourself staring back at you."

That was when I realized I'd allowed myself to fall in love with two men. While I saw a piece of myself staring back at me from Jessie's eyes, it was no match to the giant piece looking back from Asher's penetrating gaze.

"You kept something from me that affected *me* directly," I continue.

"How was I supposed to know you wanted to reconcile with him? According to what both you and Jessie told me about the fight you had before Christmas break, it seemed you'd written him off. Hell, he said you tried to give back the ring, but he begged you to keep it."

"All the more reason he shouldn't have sought out his ex," I snip back.

"Agreed, but you also can't stand there and blame me for this. I figured you were so adamant about seeing Jessie so you could officially end this chapter, not start a new one." He shakes his head, swallowing hard. "I didn't even stop to consider you might still want to be with him after refusing to talk to him all of Christmas break."

"Maybe you should have," I say in a shaky voice. "Like you should have thought about telling me what you knew about Jessie."

"I *did* think about it, goddammit!" He slams his hand into the wall, frustration radiating from his fist, spreading up his tense arm and through the rest of his body. "I'm not saying what Jessie did was right, but he was in a really bad place. I wanted to tell you Candace had started circling like a hawk again." His head hangs as he expels a breath.

"Then why didn't you?"

It's not the fact that he kept this from me that has betrayal flowing through my body. Once I'd realized my feelings for Asher, I knew I could never be with Jessie again. It's the realization of the truth that's been screaming at me ever since I first felt myself falling victim to Asher's hypnotic spell. Since I realized I'd fallen in love with him all those years ago.

He will *always* choose Jessie. I shouldn't be surprised. And I can't blame him for it. They're brothers. Family. I'm no one.

"Jessie's my brother." His voice is choked as he brings his eyes back to mine. "I couldn't betray him like that."

All I can do is nod at his confirmation of my suspicion, the lump in my throat bordering on painful, cutting off my oxygen. This is the reason I walked away all those years ago. And the reason I should have walked away the other night at the bar. There is no possible way for us to have a happy ending. Not when it means hurting someone we both love. And despite it all, I do still love Jessie. At least the Jessie he was when we dated.

A loud chiming cuts through the tension, causing Asher to flinch. I have no reason to believe it, other than a feeling in my gut, but I know the alert is a text from Jessie. I don't say a word, just glance at the outline of a cellphone in Asher's pocket. I can tell he's struggling between staying in the moment with me and seeing what his brother wants. When it chimes again, he groans, yanking it out.

"You should go," I say softly, turning from him. "Distract him. I'll finish packing and be out of your way so you don't have to keep him hidden."

"Please, Izzy. I don't want to leave you like this. What can I do to make up for it? I'll do anything."

I glance over my shoulder as I'm about to disappear into the bathroom. "We both know there's nothing you can do. Jessie will always come between us. We were fooling ourselves to hope otherwise."

"He doesn't have to. We don't have to let him."

I force a smile, although my heart is breaking. I step toward him, a breath away. "I think you already have."

He parts his lips, but I place a finger over his mouth, silencing him. Then I hoist myself onto my toes, kissing him one last time. A lone tear slides down my cheek at the finality of it all. He senses it, too, his chin quivering.

"Goodbye, Asher." Lowering myself to my heels, I walk into the bathroom, closing the door behind me. It's silent for a moment, not so much as the rustling of his clothes or shuffling of his feet across the carpet.

Then his phone chimes again, the sound striking against the stillness.

"Fuck," he groans, his footsteps loud as he storms out of the room, slamming the door. I remain still for several long moments, unsure if Asher's frustration is aimed at me or Jessie. I get the feeling it's the latter.

Just when I'm about to head back into the bedroom to finish packing, I hear the door open once more. I freeze, barely breathing. Soft footsteps pad into the room and stop for a moment. Maybe two. Then they retreat, the door opening and closing again.

I wait a few minutes to see if he returns. When he doesn't, I peek into the room. Confirming I'm alone, I hurry to the bedroom door and lock it before heading to my suitcase to finish packing. As I approach, I stop in my tracks. On top of my haphazardly packed clothes sits an origami dove.

A soft smile pulls on my lips as I pick it up, examining it. It's something we did whenever we got into an argument, which usually revolved around Jessie. It was our way of apologizing to each other. Our way of reconciling.

I don't think that's in the cards anymore.

Once I'm dressed and all my things are shoved into my suitcase, I request an Uber, praying the service isn't down as an aftereffect of the blackout. Thankfully, it goes through. I fire off a quick text to Chloe to let her know.

> Requested an Uber. Will be here in ten. Meet me by the front gate.

All I can do is hope she's awake. Worst-case scenario, she can find her own way to the airport.

When my phone buzzes, I glance at the screen.

> *Okay. Just packing up.*

Shoving it into my purse, I do one last check of the room. Apart from the mussed-up sheets, it looks exactly as it did yesterday when I first stepped over the threshold, blown away by the posh surroundings. Longing fills me at everything I lost in the past twenty-four hours. Then again, two days ago, I never expected to see Asher York. I'll just forget I saw him. Leave whatever happened in this godforsaken city.

My bags in hand, I open the door and step into the hallway, pausing to listen for any indication that Jessie may be in one of the common areas. Thankfully, I don't hear him. I don't hear anything.

With quick steps, I make my way to the lower level as quietly as possible, keeping my eyes forward as I dash toward the front door. The second I'm outside, I exhale, my muscles relaxing. This scenario reminds me of having to sneak out of my high school boyfriend's house when his parents unexpectedly returned from a weekend trip before either of us anticipated. But this is worse. I knew who I was running from then. Now, I'm not sure.

I head down the walkway, slipping out of the open gate, and peer down the street for our car. Within moments, I sense Chloe approach.

"Hey, Iz."

"Hey, Chloe." I shift my eyes to hers, smiling a small smile. She doesn't have to say a word. I can tell things between Lincoln and her ended as spectacularly as between Asher and me. And she can probably sense there were quite a few fireworks on our end this morning.

We both shrug at the same time and say, "Vegas."

Our laughter surrounds us as we hug each other. This is what I need right now. To laugh with one of my oldest friends. To feel her understanding. To give her the comfort she needs, too.

"So you're not going to see him again," I state.

She pulls away. "What choice do I have?"

I nod, more than aware of her reasoning for not wanting to see Lincoln again, even if they do live in the same city. She's so used to people disappointing her, she assumes no one would want to be with her if they knew about her mother.

"You're not going to see him again?" she asks after a beat.

I face her, my eyes brimming with tears. I could finally tell her the truth of what really happened all those years ago and get her opinion. But would any of that matter? Regardless of whether Jessie actually did cheat on me, as I led everyone to believe, nothing could ever come from this thing with Asher. I'll always be his brother's ex-fiancée. As he just demonstrated, he will always choose Jessie over me. As he should. After all, I'm just someone he knew once upon a time.

"What choice do *I* have?"

Thank you for reading MIND GAMES! I hope you enjoyed this little taste of Izzy and Asher. Their full story is coming soon. Pre-order your copy of Dangerous Games today.

Asher York.
Talented musician.
The voice of an angel.
The body of an Adonis.
And the man I happened to have a one-night stand with in Vegas.

No big deal, right? What happens in Vegas... Well, you know how the saying goes.

Did I mention he's also my ex-fiancé's older brother?

I walked away, hoping my momentary lack of judgment would stay in the past.

Boy was I wrong.

Now Asher is back in my life, and that flame I'd hoped would flicker and die after our months apart still burns bright.

But can I put my heart on the line, knowing this man has the power to obliterate it? Can I allow myself to come between two brothers?

There's only one way to find out.

Let the games begin...

https://www.tkleighauthor.com/dangerous-games

Acknowledgments

I was never supposed to write this book. I know. I know. I've said that before. In all reality, the best books are those we, as authors, never saw coming. The storyline here may sound familiar, since this was the launching point of Chloe and Lincoln's story in Wicked Games. But people were curious about Izzy and Asher. So at the end of Wicked Games, I mentioned I'd be publishing Izzy and Asher's story next — Dangerous Games. Well, this isn't that. But to write Dangerous Games, I needed to go back and really figure out what happened between them during the blackout… And before then. Originally, this was just going to be a short little novella for my mailing list. But as we all know, I can't write a short book to save my life, so while I did give my mailing list a sneak peek at early chapters of this, I decided to publish this story for everyone needing a little Izzy and Asher fix while they wait for Dangerous Games to be published.

Writing a book, even a shorter book, requires an army. And I have an amazing army. A big thanks to my hubby, Stan, for putting up with my mindless ramblings as I talk about plot points, not letting him getting a single word in while I work things out. And on that same note, I couldn't do this without my two amazing nannies, Karissa and Bree, both who take care of little

169

Harper Leigh as if she were her own, allowing me time to write.

A big thanks to my amazing editor, Kim Young, who I'm sure is now used to my crazy publishing schedule, especially deciding to release a book at the last minute (like this one). She's the only woman I've ever trusted with my book babies and I couldn't be happier to have found her.

To all my blackout girls... Why am I still writing about this dang blackout? This is the last blackout story. I hope... But honestly, this blackout is the reason there is an Asher and Izzy. And I couldn't imagine not having an Asher and Izzy. So thank you!

Thanks to my incredibly amazing PA, Melissa Crump. Dude. You da best. I'd be lost without you. Or at least have a lot more gray hair than I already do. Love you.

Another big thanks to my betas. I know I didn't have you read this one, but thanks for NOT reading it even though I'm sure you're salivating for your Izzy and Asher fix. But I need your eyes fresh and minds blank for Dangerous Games.

To my BFF A.D. Justice... This author biz would suck without your honest feedback about everything. (And thanks for telling me I'm not crazy for wanting to change titles.)

To my fabulous admins... Thanks for keeping everything under control while I hide away and write.

To my review group — thank you so much for taking the time and reading all my books before release. Your passion and commitment to reading and supporting not only me, but so many other authors, is truly humbling and inspiring.

Last but not least, thanks to you for picking up this book and taking a chance on me. I hope you've enjoyed this little taste of Izzy and Asher. Their "real" story is coming very soon.

Peace & love,

~ T.K

Books by T.K. Leigh

ROMANTIC SUSPENSE
The Beautiful Mess Series
A Beautiful Mess
A Tragic Wreck
Gorgeous Chaos
Chasing the Dragon (Deception Duet #1)
Slaying the Dragon (Deception Duet #2)
Vanished: A Beautiful Mess Series Novel

The Vault
Inferno

Heart of Light

CONTEMPORARY ROMANCE
The Redemption Series
Promise: A Redemption Series Prologue
Commitment
Redemption

The Dating Games Series
Dating Games
Wicked Games
Mind Games
Dangerous Games
Royal Games

ROMANTIC COMEDY
The Other Side of Someday
Writing Mr. Right

MATURE YOUNG ADULT
Heart of Marley

For more information on any of these titles and upcoming releases, please visit T.K.'s website:
www.tkleighauthor.com

About the Author

T.K. Leigh, otherwise known as Tracy Leigh Kellam, is the *USA Today* Bestselling author of the Beautiful Mess series, in addition to several other works ranging from sexy and sinful to fun and flirty. Originally from New England, she now resides in sunny Southern California with her husband, beautiful daughter, and three cats. When she's not planted in front of her computer, writing away, she can be found training for her next marathon (of which she has run over twenty fulls and far too many halfs to recall) or chasing her daughter around the house.

T.K. Leigh is represented by Jane Dystel of Dystel, Goderich & Bourret Literary Management. All publishing inquiries, including audio, foreign, and film rights, should be directed to her.

Made in United States
North Haven, CT
12 July 2024

54740740R00109